The Woman with the Wolf

RENÉE VIVIEN

The Woman with the Wolf

ENGLISH TRANSLATION

EDITED BY

Melanie Hawthorne

TRANSLATED BY

Karla Jay and Yvonne M. Klein

TRANSLATION REVISED BY

Melanie Hawthorne

The Modern Language Association of America

New York 2021

Printed in the United States of America

Library of Congress Cataloging-in-Publication Data

Names: Vivien, Renée, 1877–1909, author. | Hawthorne, Melanie, editor. | Jay, Karla, translator. | Klein, Yvonne, translator.
Title: The woman with the wolf / Renée Vivien ; edited by Melanie Hawthorne ; translated by Karla Jay and Yvonne M. Klein ; translation revised by Melanie Hawthorne.
Other titles: Dame à la louve. English
Description: New York : Modern Language Association of America, 2021. | Series: Texts and translations, 1079-2538 ; 36 | Includes bibliographical references. | Summary: "An English translation of short stories by Renée Vivien (1877–1909). Reflects and challenges attitudes of the belle epoque, questions gender roles, and represents same-sex love and desire. Stories feature unreliable narrators and include rewritten fairy tales and ancient myths, adventure stories in the American West and at sea, and others"—Provided by publisher.
Identifiers: LCCN 2021009007 (print) | LCCN 2021009008 (ebook) | ISBN 9781603295277 (paperback) | ISBN 9781603295284 (EPUB)
Subjects: LCSH: Vivien, Renée, 1877–1909—Translations into English. | France—Social life and customs—Fiction. | LCGFT: Short stories.
Classification: LCC PQ2643.I9 D3513 2021 (print) | LCC PQ2643.I9 (ebook) | DDC 843/.914—dc23
LC record available at https://lccn.loc.gov/2021009007
LC ebook record available at https://lccn.loc.gov/2021009008

Texts and Translations 36

ISSN 1079-2538

Cover illustration: Pacific Mail Line postcard, early twentieth century, personal collection of Melanie Hawthorne.

Published by The Modern Language Association of America
85 Broad Street, Suite 500, New York, New York 10004-2434
www.mla.org

Contents

Introduction

Renée Vivien was born Pauline Mary Tarn, the daughter of a well-to-do English gentleman and his American wife, in London in 1877. "Renée Vivien" is just one of several pseudonyms she later chose, but it is the best-known. Vivien's family moved from London to Paris when she was still an infant, so she grew up bilingual and France became her adopted home, although after her father died in 1886 she was forced to return to London with her mother until she came of age and could decide for herself where to settle.[1]

As the female child of an upper-class family at the turn of the century, Vivien did not receive formal schooling. Her education came from private governesses, from reading widely (we have some indication of her tastes from the books that belonged to her), and from the exposure to culture that comes with affluence: travel, easy access to concerts and exhibitions, and socializing with the elite.[2] Her education, intended to prepare her for the marriage market, included subjects considered social graces, such as the study of music, but omitted those her male peers would have taken for granted, such as Latin and Greek (and, unlike Virginia Woolf, she had no brothers to learn from). Vivien later hired her own tutor, learned Greek well enough to be able to translate it (Sappho would be a huge influence on her work), and taught herself to read other languages, such as Italian.[3] But in her adolescent years, like other girls of her generation, she did what was expected of her: she "came out" as a debutante into London society and was presented to Queen Victoria.

Once Vivien turned twenty-one, as an heiress, she had the means to maintain her independence and her own residence, so she returned to the wealthy neighborhood where she had grown up, near the Arc de Triomphe in Paris, and lived for the rest of her life on the same site she had inhabited as a child, the Avenue du Bois de Boulogne, now the Avenue Foch. She also had the means to travel, and she took full advantage, visiting fashionable resorts as the seasons dictated (Nice for the carnival in spring; the Bayreuth Festival in Germany; various spas) and also taking in more far-flung destinations (Constantinople, Japan). But Paris remained her home base until her death. Economically privileged, she could have chosen a life of leisure and indulgence, but she instead imposed upon herself a rigorous program of study (Greek, French poetic metrics) and writing, publishing some twenty-five books in the decade from 1901 to 1910. She financed publication herself and did not need to concern herself with sales or critical reception, though she was pleased when noticed. Her oeuvre consists mainly of poetry and short stories, though she also published two versions of an autobiographical novel, a volume of Japanese- and Chinese-inspired folk stories, and translations of Greek women poets, among other works (see Bac).

Vivien flourished in the belle epoque world of turn-of-the-century Paris. The period from 1895 to the outbreak of World War I was marked by relative political stability and French cultural dominance (see Winock). After a century of upheavals—from the Revolution of 1789 until the Franco-Prussian War and its aftermath, the Commune, in 1870–71—in which every generation had witnessed a major political conflict, France was at last enjoying a period of relative calm, particularly once the anarchist terrorism of the 1890s had subsided. Even as the polarizing Dreyfus Affair divided the country in two and exposed an ugly vein of anti-Semitism that prefigured the later rise of fascism, Paris beckoned to the world as the center of innovation in technology and the arts.[4] A series of world exhibitions, culminating in the Paris Exposition of 1900, brought the world to the capital to see its post-Haussmann beauty[5] enhanced by modern lighting and new landmarks, such as the Eiffel Tower, and showcased French ingenuity and industrial leadership.[6] Cinema, credited as the invention of the Lumière brothers in 1895, was spreading rapidly as a form of popular entertainment by the first decades of the twentieth century, and the invention of the motorcar (Peugeot was an early French manufacturer) offered new distractions and discoveries. The development of railway networks brought the middle classes from the provinces to Paris while offering an escape for Parisians who wanted to get away to the coast. Cabarets and casual drinking establishments entertained just about everyone, department stores (the source of the Tarn family wealth) offered a new kind of consumer experience, and industry provided new devices and inventions, from telephones to indoor plumbing, that benefited every household (see Weber; Rearick). Although the term *belle epoque* was used only in retrospect (see Kalifa), there was a widespread feeling that it was a beautiful time to be alive in the world-class capital of Paris, at least for those who could partake in some of its luxuries.

Money does not guarantee happiness, however, and Vivien's personal life was far from contented. The most salient factor was her sexuality, since from an early age she knew she was attracted to women and had no interest in men, marriage, or children, the socially prescribed features of a woman's life at this time. Although homosexuality had been decriminalized since the French Revolution, and belle epoque Paris was somewhat tolerant of lesbianism in certain contexts (among courtesans, for example), such behavior was far from being completely accepted, and Vivien found certain doors closed to her.[7] While protected to some extent by her wealth and social standing, she was keenly aware of her outsider status. Many of her poems describe her sense of being pilloried and vilified, and she believed that her lifestyle as an independent woman, a lesbian, and an aspiring writer represented a form of martyrdom.

The great love of Vivien's life was the expatriate American heiress Natalie Barney, with whom Vivien began a tempestuous affair in the winter of 1899–1900.[8] It was a whirlwind romance that would inspire many of Vivien's greatest poems, but Barney was not the sort of person to settle down in domestic bliss, and neither was Vivien, although she expected greater fidelity than Barney was prepared to offer. It is difficult to say when the affair ended, since there were numerous ruptures and reunions, but by 1903 Vivien was involved in a new relationship. This was with a scion of the Rothschild family, Hélène de Zuylen, who was married with children and not about to give up her social position. Fortunately, she lived nearby, on the same avenue as Vivien, which facilitated their meetings.

The relationship with de Zuylen provided some peace and stability, if not exactly happiness, for Vivien while she came to terms with the death of her closest friend, Violet Shillito. A childhood neighbor, friend, and soul sister, Shillito had perhaps helped Vivien become aware of her sapphic inclinations, though the two probably were not lovers. It was Shillito who introduced Vivien to Barney. Shillito died in Cannes of typhoid fever in 1901, at the age of twenty-four.

She made a deathbed request to see Vivien one last time, but the latter was being swept off her feet by Barney and delayed the journey. She finally arrived in Cannes to see Shillito before she died but experienced lingering guilt about the betrayal. Vivien also seems to have idealized the friendship in retrospect, and the violet (the color, the flower, the perfume) is the most obsessively recurrent single image throughout her work.

After breaking up with de Zuylen in about 1905, Vivien went into a downward emotional spiral. She had manifested suicidal tendencies as an adolescent; appeared anorexic throughout her life; seemed to survive on a liquid, alcohol diet; and depended heavily on medicinal drugs (opiate-based home remedies were barely regulated and widely available, for example [see Inglis]). In the final years of her life, Vivien seemed caught up in a frenetic circle of partying and casual affairs while inwardly withdrawing from the world in ascetic detachment, an imbalance that caught up with her in 1909. She died in November of that year after a protracted illness, at the age of thirty-two. Scholars continue to debate the exact cause of her early death and whether or not it constitutes a suicide. Whatever the verdict, her demise robbed the world of a fiercely independent and unique voice.

The full range of that talent is on display in the stories that comprise *La dame à la louve* (*The Woman with the Wolf*). Originally published in 1904, when Vivien was at the height of her powers, it brings together a range of themes and forms that show many facets of the author's work. The opening story, which gives the collection its title, is a masterful example of the short story genre that calls out for comparison to Anton Chekhov's "Lady with Lapdog" while also offering a coded representation of same-sex love through the example of a strange commitment that seems inexplicable to the world at large. The narrative takes place on a passenger ship that hits a reef. The narrator of this story simply cannot fathom why the lady he has his eye on would choose to drown with her pet wolf rather than take the seat that's offered in the lifeboat, but to the reader it is all too clear. Vivien's story anticipates the real-life tragedy of the *Titanic*, and her story is titanic in the original sense of the word through its force and power.

Several stories in the collection offer reworkings of well-known fairy stories, such as the Prince Charming who turns out to be a young woman, or the heroine who would rather swallow a frog than kiss a prince (or a man who sees himself as one). These "fractured fairytales" anticipate the ways later writers such as the British postmodernist Angela Carter would reappropriate popular narratives to show a different point of view, one that embraces risk and danger and rewrites female desire as a force that disrupts comfortable certainties.

Other stories in *The Woman with the Wolf* range from predictable decadent themes about jewels and women's virtue in the face of male depravity, such as "Le voile de Vasthi" ("The Veil of Vashti"), to more original and surprising stories set in the wilds of the United States, such as "Brune comme une noisette" ("The Nut-Brown Maid") or "La soif ricane" ("Sniggering Thirst"), which describes a terrifying wildfire on the prairie. These themes resonate with both fin de siècle and modern preoccupations, offering new perspectives and even flashes of humor.

Whatever the theme, however, these stories all share a questioning of gender and gender roles. Vivien's understanding of sex, gender, and sexuality differed in its assumptions from contemporary theory, yet it converges with modern perspectives in challenging normative views and moral hypocrisy. In some ways, then, Vivien was ahead of her time, though in other ways she can be seen as a product of it.

In general, the belle epoque was a time of rapid gains in rights for women (see Moses; Offen; Scott). In the last two decades of the nineteenth century, when Vivien was growing up, the government of the Third Republic had passed a number of reforms, allowing divorce, mandating girls' education, and opening up the professions, and the belle epoque would see further reforms. Although the vote remained elusive in France until 1944, women could bring paternity suits (see Fuchs) and serve as witnesses in legal trials in the first decade of the twentieth century. And exceptional women such as Marie Curie challenged stereotypes about what women could and couldn't do through their spectacular success: Curie not only won two Nobel prizes—the first during Vivien's lifetime, in 1903—but won them in two different categories, physics and chemistry.

These and other improvements in women's status had a notable effect on the literary environment for female authors. The first decades of the twentieth century saw a remarkable increase in the number of women who not only committed their thoughts to paper but also published and even made a living from their work. Rising literacy rates in the nineteenth century combined with technical developments in printing and improved access to education for girls meant that there was finally a market for women's work, be it journalism or fiction, and there was a veritable explosion of writing by women (see Holmes and Tarr; Rogers; and Waelti-Walters).

Vivien and her contemporaries had inherited the Victorian paradigm that men and women were very different creatures, but they challenged the conclusion that they should remain in separate spheres. The perception of women as governed by emotion and more sensitive than men disqualified women in some minds from participating in public life but impressed others, including Vivien, as evidence of women's superiority to men. According to this argument, women deserved the vote and greater influence in politics because they were more moral than men (they resisted vices such as drinking and whoring), not because they were like men (the basis of the modern argument against sex discrimination). Such attitudes linked feminism at the turn of the century to other social movements such as the temperance cause, prison reform, abolitionism, public education, and nascent social welfare programs (such as assistance for "fallen women," i.e., prostitutes, and for single mothers). The flip side of this argument could lead to prudery, puritanism, and all kinds of antipleasure, antisex rhetoric—arguments revived in the second wave of the women's movement in the 1970s and '80s, when radical feminists sometimes found themselves on the same side as the so-called moral majority of conservatives in debates around pornography and transgender issues (see Echols).

Since Vivien held such beliefs, she may not have found promoting androgyny or blurring gender boundaries to be desirable goals. Men might be enviable for their access to educational, cultural, and professional opportunities; their ability to court women openly; and their self-determination, but Vivien was of her time in thinking of men and women as two different forms (dimorphism) rather than as one species existing on a continuum. Many have latched onto the photographs of Vivien dressed as a late-eighteenth-century man standing next to Barney in a skimpy Empire dress, asserting that Vivien made a habit of cross-dressing, but such costumes were part of a playful repertoire of dressing up for costume balls, and there is no evidence to suggest that Vivien ever cross-dressed aside from these rare occasions when such cosplay (as it is now referred to in popular culture) was accepted. True, she experimented with switching genders and seeing things from a man's point of view, but only in limited contexts, including her fiction. She explored alternative female identities too (she was photographed as Anne Boleyn and in a Turkish costume with a veil), but such alter egos were experimental only. In Vivien's eyes, to become a man would have been aiming low, but to expand the freedom of women into male-dominated territory was a worthy goal.

That said, Vivien's fiction lends itself well to a critique of gender roles from a modern (and literary modernist) point of view. The short stories in *The Woman with the Wolf* ask us to question what is really masculine and what is really feminine. In the title story, for example, the male passengers panic and flee to the lifeboats when the ship hits the reef, while the woman remains calm and stoic. Perhaps Vivien had in mind the fire at an annual charity event in Paris in 1897 that killed 125 people, most of them women from the aristocracy. The event was a scandal not only because of the death toll among the elite but also because so many men escaped, abandoning the women they were supposed to protect. In "The Woman with the Wolf," Vivien depicts the male passengers as cowardly, even hysterical, while the heroine faces death calmly and remains loyal to her companion, not leaving her to die alone.

The title story also questions assumptions about male privilege in ways that chime with the contemporary Me Too movement: the man expects the woman to talk with him simply because he feels like talking to her, and takes even a direct "no" as a sign of encouragement. Vivien's presentations of women who chafe at restrictive gender expectations and men who take their privilege for granted are every bit as relevant today, and many women who have ever traveled alone will be able to put themselves in the heroine's shoes.

In her own travels, and at home in cosmopolitan Paris, Vivien mingled with people of different races and religions (she had an affair with the wife of a Turkish—i.e., Muslim—diplomat, and Barney was part Jewish) if they were wealthy enough to be her social equals. In her fiction, however, Vivien tends to take stereotypes as the starting point for engaging with other cultures and races. Thus, although she collected art from China and Japan, and traveled through Asia on a cruise in 1907, the stories she sets there (for example, in the short story collection *Netsuké*) appear on the surface to rely on conventional thinking about these countries. Her Chinese and Japanese girls ("mousmés") appear demure and modest (though are capable of great strength and defiance when motivated); the culture can seem cruel and the etiquette arcane. Her stories set in the prairies and backwoods of America, another exotic setting for European readers, likely bear the imprint of her mother's own childhood in the small town of Jackson, Michigan, still considered by white settlers in the mid–nineteenth century to be part of the western "frontier." The so-called Indian Wars were still being fought to the west and southwest (conflicts continued well into the twentieth century), and the doctrine of Manifest Destiny—that the country was meant to belong to white settlers by divine intention—provided a convenient ideological alibi for the dominant view that "Indians" (lumped together regardless of individual tribe) represented obstacles to expansion and therefore could and should be removed and dispossessed.[9]

Perhaps Vivien had her own reasons for invoking these commonplaces, and more study is needed to understand and appreciate the extent of those intentions (see, for example, Hawthorne, "Behind the Bamboo Screen"). But she was not alone in approaching other cultures primarily through stereotypes; events such as the great Paris Exhibition of 1900 encouraged the public to think in these terms. The exhibition re-created what were touted as authentic "street scenes" as a form of popular spectacle, and for many this was their introduction to other parts of the world. The stories in *The Woman with the Wolf* often begin with such clichéd settings, quickly sketched, and it is easy to call out the stereotypes. On closer inspection, however, many stories go on to present a more unconventional and often disturbing perspective: an Egyptian woman with skin like a crocodile, a biblical queen we thought we knew who reveals inner depths, a Greek heroine whose secret desire, never before questioned, catches us by surprise. The invitation to look deeper than what seems obvious on the surface is a recurrent theme that should be kept in mind when addressing Vivien's apparently conformist attitudes on matters of nationality and race.

The present translation is a revised version of the 1983 edition originally published by Gay Presses of New York. It is a reminder that Vivien's memory was kept alive during the twentieth century by a subculture of feminists and lesbians who valued her work and sought it out in translation (especially as the original French was not always readily available). The first books about her, such as André Germain's *Renée Vivien*, began appearing soon after her death. Within a generation or two she was incorporated into the lesbian canon in the United States through the work of Jeannette Foster, the first librarian of Alfred Kinsey's Institute for Sex Research, who compiled the pioneering study *Sex Variant*

Women in Literature, one of the first attempts to inventory the presence of nonheteronormative women in literature.

Renewed interest in feminism and women's literature was part of the second wave of the women's movement, which helped bring Vivien and her work to the attention of new readers. Much of her work was republished in France, along with an appreciation of her life and work by Paul Lorenz in 1977, and in 1986 she was the subject of the first and most thorough biography to date, *Tes blessures sont plus douces que leurs caresses: Vie de Renée Vivien* (*Your Wounds Are Sweeter Than Their Caresses: The Life of Renée Vivien*), by Jean-Paul Goujon.

Translations of Vivien's books began to appear in English in the 1970s (individual poems had been published in the underground lesbian magazine *The Ladder*), making her work available to anglophone critics. Her work was an inspiration to scholars as diverse as Gayle Rubin ("Introduction"), whose essay on the "traffic" in women was one of the most influential theoretical texts of second-wave feminism, and the collaborative duo Sandra Gilbert and Susan Gubar, whose hugely influential books *The Madwoman in the Attic* and the monumental, three-volume *No Man's Land: The Place of the Woman Writer in the Twentieth Century* set the new paradigm for feminist literary scholarship. (Renée Vivien was also one of the principal figures in Susan Gubar's freestanding article "Sapphistries.") The pioneer of lesbian studies Karla Jay wrote the first book in English devoted to Vivien, *The Amazon and the Page: Natalie Clifford Barney and Renée Vivien*, and was responsible, with Yvonne Klein, for the first translation of *La dame à la louve*, the basis of the present text (see Vivien, *Woman*).

Interest in Vivien continued steadily throughout the 1990s and beyond. A major poetic study in French by Virginie

Sanders appeared in 1991, Mireille Rosello included Vivien in her book on women's writing in 1996, and a series of significant articles by Tama Lea Engelking begins in the early 1990s and continues into the present ("Decadence," "Genre," "One Hundred Years," "Renée Vivien," "Renée Vivien's Sapphic Legacy"). In 1994, Greta Schiller directed the film *Woman of the Wolf* based on Vivien's work. In the twenty-first century, anglophone critics of French poetry with an interest in women's poetry have recognized Vivien's centrality, as evidenced in work by Gayle Levy, Gretchen Schultz, and Sarah Parker, and a new translation of a selection of Vivien's poetry by Samantha Pious, *A Crown of Violets*, appeared in 2015. Two monographs on Vivien were published in France in the first decade of the twenty-first century (Perrin; Bartholomot Bessou), and the centenary of Vivien's death in 2009 sparked renewed interest, leading to two volumes of critical essays edited by the leading Vivien scholar Nicole Albert (*Renée Vivien à rebours* [*Renée Vivien against the Grain*] and, in collaboration with Brigitte Rollet, *Renée Vivien*), addressing all aspects of Vivien's life and work. A small, independent press, ÉrosOnyx, is in the process of republishing her entire oeuvre in France, including not only the better-known works but also juvenilia (*Le langage des fleurs* [*The Language of Flowers*]) and works that were originally published under other pseudonyms (such as *L'être double* [*Double Life*], which first appeared under the name Paule Riversdale), editions that benefit from the scholarship of Albert. Works in queer studies in the United States increasingly recognize Vivien's role as a precursor (for example, Heather Love in *Feeling Backward* and Elizabeth Freeman in *Time Binds*).

The moment has come for Vivien's work to stand once again before a wider audience with a new perspective. The times call for a renewed appreciation of voices that speak of difference; of the value of multiple perspectives that bring those previously consigned to the margins into the discussion; and of the need to reframe sexual and gender categories in terms of fluidity. All three of these discourses add nuances that inform and enrich human life. Renée Vivien's unique voice has much to offer to these and other debates.

Notes

1. For biographical information about Renée Vivien, see Goujon. In English, see Jay. For more on Vivien's American roots, see Hawthorne, "Des antécédents."

2. For a list of Vivien's books, see Albert and Rollet 185–94. Vivien's mother met the writer Anthony Trollope socially while in Hawaii, for example, and later corresponded with him.

3. Leontis provides context for women's study of the classics at the turn of the century, arguing that "women made Greek learning a sign of their capacity for cultivation" (10).

4. On the Dreyfus Affair, see for example Bredin; Begley. On the French roots of fascism, see Sternhell.

5. Georges-Eugène Haussmann was charged with redesigning and modernizing Paris during the Second Empire and is largely responsible for the city's elegant appearance today.

6. See, for example, Schivelbusch, *Disenchanted Night* and *The Railway Journey*.

7. On the history of homosexuality in France, see Huas; Lever; and Schultz, *Sapphic Fathers*; Merrick and Ragan; and Merrick and Sibalis. On the representation of lesbianism at the turn of the century, see Albert, *Lesbian Decadence*. Decriminalization did not mean total freedom from prosecution. Laws dealing with the corruption of minors and *outrage aux bonnes moeurs* (offenses against good morals, usually taken to mean sex in public) could be invoked selectively to rein in homosexual behavior.

8. On Natalie Barney, see Chalon; Rodriguez; Souhami; and Wickes.

9. Consider these historical "bookends" to Vivien's own life. General Custer's "last stand," an event we might reframe today but that passed unquestionably for heroism at the time, was in 1876, just a year

before Vivien was born. And the Apache chief Geronimo died the same year as Vivien herself, 1909. His obituary in *The New York Times* stated that he had "a reputation for cruelty and cunning never surpassed by that of any other American Indian chief" and quoted General Nelson A. Miles, who described him as "one of the lowest and most cruel of the savages of the American continent" ("Old Apache Chief"). Such attitudes were common. For more on Vivien's American heritage, see Hawthorne, "Des antécédents."

Works Cited

Albert, Nicole G. *Lesbian Decadence: Representations in Art and Literature of Fin-de-siècle France.* Translated by Nancy Erber and William K. Peniston, Harrington Park Press, 2016.

———, editor. *Renée Vivien à rebours: Études pour un centenaire.* Orizons, 2009.

Albert, Nicole G., and Brigitte Rollet, editors. *Renée Vivien: Une femme de lettres entre deux siècles, 1877–1909.* Champion, 2012.

Bac, Claude. *Renée Vivien: Inventaire raisonné des livres publiés de 1901 à 1948.* 2003.

Bartholomot Bessou, Marie-Ange. *L'imaginaire du féminin dans l'oeuvre de Renée Vivien.* PU Blaise Pascal, 2004.

Begley, Louis. *Why the Dreyfus Affair Matters.* Yale UP, 2009.

Bredin, Jean-Denis. *The Affair: The Case of Alfred Dreyfus.* Translated by Jeffrey Mehlman, Braziller, 1986.

Carter, Angela. *The Bloody Chamber.* Gollancz, 1979.

Chalon, Jean. *Portrait of a Seductress: The World of Natalie Barney.* Translated by Carol Barko, Crown, 1979.

Chekhov, Anton. "Lady with Lapdog." *"Lady with Lapdog" and Other Stories*, translated by David Magarshack, Penguin, 1964, pp. 264–81.

Echols, Alice. *Daring to be Bad: Radical Feminism in America, 1967–1975.* U of Minnesota P, 1989.

Engelking, Tama Lea. "Decadence and the Woman Writer: Renée Vivien's *Une femme m'apparut.*" Holmes and Tarr, pp. 225–37.

———. "Genre and the Mark of Gender: Renée Vivien's 'Sonnet féminin.'" *Modern Language Studies*, vol. 23, no. 4, Autumn 1993, pp. 79–92.

———. "One Hundred Years of 'Imaginary Renée Viviens.'" *Women's Self-Narrative across the Francophone World*, special issue of *Women in French Studies*, 2011, pp. 52–62.

———. "Renée Vivien and the Ladies of the Lake." *Nineteenth-Century French Studies*, vol. 30, nos. 3–4, 2002, pp. 363–80, https://doi.org/10.1353/ncf.2002.0014.

———. "Renée Vivien's Sapphic Legacy: Remembering the 'House of Muses.'" *Atlantis*, vol. 18, nos. 1–2, 1992–93, pp. 125–41.

Foster, Jeannette. *Sex Variant Women in Literature*. Vantage Press, 1956.

Freeman, Elizabeth. *Time Binds: Queer Temporalities, Queer Histories*. Duke UP, 2010.

Fuchs, Rachel G. *Contested Paternity: Constructing Families in Modern France*. Johns Hopkins UP, 2008.

Germain, André. *Renée Vivien*. Crès, 1917.

Gilbert, Sandra, and Susan Gubar. *The Madwoman in the Attic*. Yale UP, 1979.

———. *No Man's Land: The Place of the Woman Writer in the Twentieth Century*. Yale UP, 1988–96. 3 vols.

Goujon, Jean-Paul. *Tes blessures sont plus douces que leurs caresses: Vie de Renée Vivien*. Régine Deforges, 1986.

Gubar, Susan. "Sapphistries." *Signs*, vol. 10, no. 1, Autumn 1984, pp. 43–62.

Hawthorne, Melanie. "Des antécédents américains de Renée Vivien." *Histoires Littéraires*, no. 66, 2016, pp. 69–74.

———. "Behind the Bamboo Screen: Renée Vivien and the Rituals of Self Destruction." *French Review*, vol. 92, no. 4, May 2019, pp. 54–66.

Holmes, Diana, and Carrie Tarr, editors. *A "Belle Époque"? Women in French Society and Culture, 1890–1914*. Berghahn, 2006.

Huas, Jeanine. *L'homosexualité au temps de Proust*. Editions Danclau, 1992.

Inglis, Lucy. *Milk of Paradise: A History of Opium*. Pegasus, 2019.

Jay, Karla. *The Amazon and the Page: Natalie Clifford Barney and Renée Vivien*. Indiana UP, 1988.

Kalifa, Dominique. *La véritable histoire de la Belle Époque*. Fayard, 2017.

Leontis, Artemis. *Eva Palmer Sikelianos: A Life in Ruins*. Princeton UP, 2019.

Lever, Maurice. *Les bûchers de Sodome: Histoire des "infâmes."* Fayard, 1985.

Levy, Gayle A. *Refiguring the Muse.* Peter Lang, 1999.

Lorenz, Paul. *Sappho 1900: Renée Vivien.* Julliard, 1977.

Love, Heather. *Feeling Backward: Loss and the Politics of Queer History.* Harvard UP, 2007.

Merrick, Jeffrey, and Bryant T. Ragan, Jr., editors. *Homosexuality in Modern France.* Oxford UP, 1996.

Merrick, Jeffrey, and Michael Sibalis, editors. "Homosexuality in French History and Culture." *Journal of Homosexuality*, vol. 41, nos. 3–4, 2001.

Moses, Claire Goldberg. *French Feminism in the Nineteenth Century.* State U of New York P, 1985.

Offen, Karen. *European Feminisms, 1700–1950: A Political History.* Stanford UP, 1999.

"Old Apache Chief Geronimo Is Dead." *The New York Times*, 18 Feb. 1909, archive.nytimes.com/www.nytimes.com/learning/general/onthisday/bday/0616.html.

Parker, Sarah. *The Lesbian Muse and Poetic Identity, 1889–1930.* Routledge, 2015.

Perrin, Marie. *Renée Vivien, le corps exsangue: De l'anorexie mentale à la création littéraire.* L'Harmattan, 2003.

Rearick, Charles. *Pleasures of the Belle Epoque: Entertainment and Festivity in Turn-of-the-Century France.* Yale UP, 1986.

Rodriguez, Suzanne. *Wild Heart: A Life: Natalie Clifford Barney's Journey from Victorian American to the Literary Salons of Paris.* HarperCollins, 2002.

Rogers, Juliette M. *Career Stories: Belle Epoque Novels of Professional Development.* Penn State UP, 2008.

Rosello, Mireille. *Infiltrating Culture: Power and Identity in Contemporary Women's Writing.* Manchester UP, 1996.

Rubin, Gayle S. *Deviations: A Gayle Rubin Reader.* Duke UP, 2011.

———. "Introduction to *A Woman Appeared to Me.*" Rubin, *Deviations*, pp. 87–108.

———. "The Traffic in Women: Notes on the 'Political Economy' of Sex." Rubin, *Deviations*, pp. 33–65.

Sanders, Virginie. *"Vertigineusement, j'allais vers les Étoiles . . .": La poésie de Renée Vivien, 1877–1909*. Rodopi, 1991.

Schivelbusch, Wolfgang. *Disenchanted Night: The Industrialization of Light in the Nineteenth Century*. U of California P, 1988.

———. *The Railway Journey: The Industrialization of Time and Space in the Nineteenth Century*. U of California P, 1986.

Schultz, Gretchen, editor. *An Anthology of Nineteenth-Century Women's Poetry from France*. Modern Language Association of America, 2008.

———. *Sapphic Fathers: Discourses of Same-Sex Desire from Nineteenth-Century France*. Toronto UP, 2014.

Scott, Joan Wallach. *Only Paradoxes to Offer: French Feminists and the Rights of Man*. Harvard UP, 1996.

Souhami, Diana. *Wild Girls: Paris, Sappho and Art: The Lives and Loves of Natalie Barney and Romaine Brooks*. Weidenfeld and Nicolson, 2004.

Sternhell, Zeev. *The Roots of Fascist Ideology: From Cultural Rebellion to Political Revolution*. Princeton UP, 1994.

Vivien, Renée. *A Crown of Violets*. Translated by Samantha Pious, Headmistress Press, 2015.

——— [*published as* Paule Riversdale]. *L'être double*. 1904. Edited by Nicolas Berger, Éditions ÉrosOnyx, 2014.

——— [*published as* Pauline Tarn]. *Le langage des fleurs*. Éditions ÉrosOnyx, 2012.

———. *"The Woman of the Wolf" and Other Stories*. Translated by Karla Jay and Yvonne M. Klein, Gay Presses of New York, 1983.

Waelti-Walters, Jennifer. *Feminist Novelists of the Belle Epoque: Love as a Lifestyle*. Indiana UP, 1990.

Weber, Eugen. *France: Fin de Siècle*. Harvard UP, 1986.

Wickes, George. *The Amazon of Letters: The Life and Loves of Natalie Barney*. Putnam, 1976.

Winock, Michel. *La belle époque*. Perrin, 2003.

Woman of the Wolf. Directed by Greta Schiller, featuring Alex Kingston, Jezebel Productions, 1994.

Suggestions for Further Reading

Beer, Thomas. *The Mauve Decade: American Life at the End of the Nineteenth Century*. Knopf, 1926.

Blankley, Elyse. "Return to Mytilène: Renée Vivien and the City of Women." *Women Writers and the City: Essays in Feminist Literary Criticism*, edited by Susan Merrill Squier, U of Tennessee P, 1984, pp. 45–67.

Bonal, Gérard. *Des Américaines à Paris, 1850–1920*. Tallandier, 2017.

Dade, Juliette. "Ineffable Gomorrah: The Performance of Lesbianism in Colette, Proust, and Vivien." *Women in French Studies*, vol. 20, 2012, pp. 9–20.

Holmes, Diana. "From the Pillory to Sappho's Island: The Poetry of Renée Vivien." *French Women's Writing, 1848–1994*, by Holmes, Athlone, 1996, pp. 83–104.

Marcus, Sharon. "Comparative Sapphism." *The Literary Channel: The Inter-national Invention of the Novel*, edited by Margaret Cohen and Carolyn Dever, Princeton UP, 2002, pp. 251–85.

Marks, Elaine. "'Sapho 1900': Imaginary Renée Viviens and the Rear of the Belle Époque." *Yale French Studies*, no. 75, 1988, pp. 175–189.

Maurras, Charles. *Le romantisme féminin*. À la cité des livres, 1926.

Renée Vivien et ses masques. Special issue of *A l'écart*, no. 2, Apr. 1980.

Vicinus, Martha. *Intimate Friends: Women Who Loved Women, 1778–1928*. U of Chicago P, 2004.

Vivien, Renée. *The Muse of the Violets.* Translated by Margaret Porter and Catharine Kroger, Naiad Press, 1977.

———. *A Woman Appeared to Me.* Translated by Jeannette H. Foster, introduction by Gayle Rubin, Naiad Press, 1976.

Note on the Translation

There are two main factors to bear in mind when considering the challenges posed by translating the prose work of Renée Vivien into English.

The first is that while French and English are closely related on the lexical plane, sharing many cognate words, the way each language encodes questions of gender is significantly different. English and French share many semantic items that derive from Greek and Latin, so that when Vivien gives one of her stories the title "La saurienne" ("The Ladysaurus"), speakers of English may easily recognize the root *-saurus* as relating to reptiles (its continuing use in popular culture to coin new character names makes the term perfectly linguistically transparent even to children). What is less clear is the morphology of the ending (*-enne* rather than *-en*) and its implications for the reader.

English grammar makes a distinction between male and female agents ("he" and "she") in relation to a perceived biological difference, allowing most substantives to remain neutral ("it"). A woman is a "she," but a wolf can be an "it." A wolf might be a "he" or a "she" if the biological sex of the creature becomes relevant (as is the case in the lead story here), but in English there is no obligation to specify either maleness or femaleness in the absence of a desire to do so.

In French, on the other hand, every noun, even the most abstract, has a grammatical gender (masculine or feminine), regardless of its biological condition, and there is no neuter, or "it." As well, adjectives must agree in form—number and gender—with the noun they modify. Gender is always on display. Consequently, there may even be moments when biological and grammatical gender are at odds: a man (*un homme*), for example, is male or masculine according to biological gender but may be referred to using a feminine noun, such as *une personne* (a person) or *une victime* (a victim), when these conditions are invoked.[1] In his article "Does Your Language Shape How You Think?" the linguist Guy Deutscher quotes Roman Jakobson, who stated, "Languages differ essentially in what they must convey and not in what they may convey." Deutscher thus proceeds to focus on what languages force us to be aware of, and in the case of French, gender is one of those things. He offers the following example:

> Suppose I say to you in English that "I spent yesterday evening with a neighbor." You may well wonder whether my companion was male or female, but I have the right to tell you politely that it's none of your business. But if we were speaking French or German, I wouldn't have the privilege to equivocate in this way, because I would be obliged by the grammar of language to choose between *voisin* or *voisine*; *Nachbar* or *Nachbarin*. These languages compel me to inform you about the sex of my companion whether or not I feel it is remotely your concern.

French obliges the speaker to think about gender in a way that English does not, and this is an issue for translators.

It is in this context of a language that forces the speaker or writer into revelations that, for example, Colette wrote her short story "Nuit blanche." The narrator describes a sleepless night in a bed that she shares with another person. She addresses the listener, her partner, directly, using the second-person singular (the *tu* ["you"] form), which is not sex-specific (unlike the third person, which distinguishes between the masculine *il* ["he"] and the feminine *elle* ["she"]), and until the last line of the story Colette avoids using any terms, such as adjectives and past participles in compound tenses, that would identify the sex of the person. Only when she finally describes her partner as "penchée" (bent over the narrator) does the grammatically feminine ending reveal the person's sex, making it clear that the couple being presented to the reader in the intimacy of their shared bedroom consists of two women.

Occasionally, the French gender system provides options that may be lacking in English, as in the case of possessive adjectives and pronouns (*yours*, *mine*, and *ours*). In English, possessive adjectives convey information about the possessor: a student who uses the pronouns *she* and *her* reads *her* book, while a student who uses the pronouns *they* and *them* reads *their* book. In French, possessive adjectives agree with the grammatical gender of the noun being owned. When a French student reads *son livre*, the adjective *son* is masculine not because of the person doing the reading, but because the noun *livre* ("book") is masculine in French. Occasionally, this system obliges translators to make gendered choices in English that were not part of the original French. "Un écrivain fait son travail" might be rendered as "a writer does *his* work," lending itself to the apparently sexist assumption that all writers are men, but such a word choice reflects the sexism of the translator, not (necessarily) the original author. While the French noun *écrivain* is grammatically masculine, it is an example of a situation where grammatical and natural gender may be at odds: *une femme* ("a woman") can be *un écrivain* in French without any sense of solecism.

Again, this situation is not without problems. As feminists have pointed out, such usage of the "universal male" can reinforce a cultural assumption that men are more likely than women to be writers or that when one thinks of writers, one thinks first (or even exclusively) of men (and not of women). In addition, sex-related bias can creep into the enterprise of translation, for example in the way translators treat sex scenes.[2] Since sex, gender, and sexual expression are at the heart of Renée Vivien's work, a feminist sensitivity to such issues is called for. There have been numerous proposals to reform the perceived sexist bias of the French language, such as the creation of feminized forms of words such as *une écrivaine* to counteract the invisibility of women effected by such universalizing language. Still, these are time-specific solutions, not universally accepted, and they were not part of the context Vivien worked in.

Even when the reader is aware of bias, gender remains a pervasive feature of French. Perhaps precisely because of the somewhat arbitrary nature of grammatical gender, French speakers are better than English speakers at not seeing gender as such a defining element of a person. After all, if *la Tour Eiffel* is a "she" and *le fromage* ("cheese") is a "he," then surely all gender has little to do with personhood. Deutscher provides an overview of some of these issues in his book *Through the Language Glass*. Reviving a version of the Sapir-Whorf hypothesis of language (the notion that language shapes how we perceive reality by structuring what we can say and think), he reviews studies that attempt to link grammatical gender in various languages to the (mostly unconscious) assumptions that speakers of those languages hold about human gender traits. Do speakers of German, for example, think of keys as "stronger" than do speakers of Spanish because the word *key* is grammatically masculine in German but feminine in Spanish? Studies quoted by

Deutscher suggest that they do (194–216), but how we interpret such data is still a matter of debate.

Deutscher cautiously concludes, "When a language treats inanimate objects in the same way as it treats women and men, with the same grammatical forms or with the same 'he' and 'she' pronouns, the habits of grammar can spill over to habits of mind beyond grammar" (214). While no one is suggesting that grammar limits higher orders of thinking (such as reasoning ability), such linguistic habits, in Deutscher's words, "may come close to being a prison-house" (215). To render Vivien's French into English may be to free it from its grammatical shackles, but speakers of English need to be aware of how the constraints would have appeared to French readers, or else they are missing an important part of the reading experience.

The second general factor to underscore is that Renée Vivien was bilingual, functioning perfectly in both English and French. She chose to express herself as a creative writer almost exclusively in French, however, and, unlike some authors (Samuel Beckett is one who comes to mind), Vivien never exercised the option to present her work in her "maternal" language, English. She never attempted to translate her own work herself, although she could easily have done so ("easily" at least in the sense of having the basic linguistic competence), nor did she seek to have it translated by someone else. We might speculate about why this was so: Did Vivien think of her audience, or her ideal reader, as French-, but not English-speaking? Did she think her work was untranslatable? Did she just not want to tackle the thorny gender issues described above? For someone attuned to gender issues, as she was, the pitfalls are daunting. We may never know the answer, but the fact that Vivien's work remained untranslated in her lifetime is cause for reflection.

Perhaps it is foolish to venture where the author herself declined to go, but if Anglophones are to enjoy a taste of Vivien's prose work, then needs must. Gender questions of the kind described above are present from the outset and have to be confronted. The very title of the collection, and of the story that sets the tone, illustrates some of the issues. The deceptively straightforward phrase "la dame à la louve"—two substantives linked by a preposition—involves so many nuances that it defies easy translation. A *dame* is a lady, somewhat higher on the social scale than the generic "woman" (*femme*), implying a degree of respect. The word *louve* illustrates the nuances of French with regard to gender, since it is the marked, feminine form of the French *loup*, a wolf (from the Latin *lupus*). French does not require that the gender of the animal be specified—a *loup* could turn out to be female—but it allows the author to specify female sex from the outset with a feminine form of the word, *louve*. English does not have this option for this animal. While there are feminine forms for cattle, deer, sheep, and pigs (cow, doe, ewe, sow), the wolf is ungendered in English. To resort to the *she-* construction (*she-wolf*), however, in accordance with the author's intention of highlighting the animal's sex, would be to sacrifice the alliterative "woman with the wolf." While it is essential to the plot that the reader remain in no doubt as to the sex of the wolf, which is crucial to understanding the choice the lady later makes, the opening conversational exchange in the story allows for the issue of the wolf's sex to come up naturally when the lady uses the pronoun *she*. Thus, the choice has been made to retain the ungendered "wolf" in the title.

Finally, there is the question of the preposition *à*. One can translate it as "with," in the sense of an attribute, something that accompanies (as apple pie is accompanied by ice cream when à la mode), and that is the choice made here. But *à* in French can mean something stronger: it can also be used to indicate possession, to convey that something belongs to someone. To pursue this thought is to notice, however, that the ownership is not of the order one might assume: it is not the wolf who belongs to the lady, but the lady who belongs to—is "à"—the wolf, an inversion of the usual master/owned relationship in addition to the sexual kind that Vivien meant to evoke in this story. If the lady cannot abandon the wolf, in the end, she does not decide freely. She is not free to choose because she belongs to the wolf; there is a unilateral dimension to the relationship that she is not in control of, that it is not within her power to abrogate. These considerations shape the choices in the translation of the title *The Woman with the Wolf*. The social nuance of "lady" is abandoned in favor of the alliterative *W*'s, the wolf's sex is revealed only in the text, and the relationship between the two is rendered as "with," a choice that avoids specifying who "belongs" to whom.

Translating the work of Renée Vivien, then, is both a straightforward and a complicated task: straightforward on a lexical level, but complicated in its nuances. For the student reader, or the general reader with a basic knowledge of French, the challenge is to appreciate that the apparent simplicity of these stories belies a radical challenge to the masculinist biases of French. These biases are enshrined in centuries of "good usage," rules and practices handed down by the venerable Académie Française (the semiofficial body charged with preserving the purity of the language) that take it as self-evident that the masculine form (of nouns, of adjectives) is the basic or unmarked form, while the feminine cannot be universal. The work of Renée Vivien asks the reader to see female experience as central, rather than marginal, and this requires an attentiveness to linguistic gender markings that may not come automatically to speakers of English (and indeed cannot always be represented in translation without heavy-handed editing). These stories handsomely repay the effort, however, and add to our understanding today of the challenges to gender relations already underway a century ago in the belle epoque (as discussed in the introduction).

The present edition is a revised version of the first English translation of *La dame à la louve*, by Karla Jay and Yvonne M. Klein, first published by the Gay Presses of New York in 1983. Capitalization and lowercasing follow the usage of the original French text. In updating the translation, I have used contracted forms ("I'm" for "I am"), followed current usage of "that" and "which," and tried to give Vivien's prose a more modern sound and rhythm for contemporary readers.

Vivien herself was a careful reader and editor, and she often made substantial last-minute changes to the proofs of her work. This tendency did not endear her to publishers, but since she paid out of pocket for their work, they accommodated her. The many emendations to the final proofs of *La dame à la louve* (in the possession of Imogen Bright, Vivien's great-niece) offer insights into how Vivien worked. Specifically, it has been suggested that they allow us to judge "du travail en profondeur que Vivien réservait à ses oeuvres, débusquant la moindre coquille, mais aussi constater, dans ce domaine comme dans d'autres, son insatisfaction permanente" 'the depth and thoroughness that Vivien saved for her own work, winkling out the tiniest mistakes, but also to notice, in this domain as in others, her permanent dissatisfaction' (Albert and Rollet 197). It is a fitting reminder that no one can ever expect to have the last word on Vivien, but also an incentive to continue to try to do justice to her work.

Notes

1. For more on the complications in French that can arise when grammatical and natural gender collide, see Ihsane and Sleeman.

2. See Flotow on the case of Simone de Beauvoir ("Translation Effects") and on feminist translation in general (*Translation and Gender*).

Works Cited

Albert, Nicole G., and Brigitte Rollet, editors. *Renée Vivien: Une femme de lettres entre deux siècles, 1877–1909.* Champion, 2012.

Colette. "Nuit blanche." *Les vrilles de la vigne,* Gallimard, 1984, pp. 969–72. Vol. 1 of *Œuvres.*

Deutscher, Guy. "Does Your Language Shape How You Think?" *The New York Times,* 26 Aug. 2010, https://nyti.ms/2k47cK3.

———. *Through the Language Glass: Why the World Looks Different in Other Languages.* Picador, 2010.

Flotow, Luise von. *Translation and Gender: Translating in the "Era of Feminism."* U of Ottawa P, 1997.

———. "Translation Effects: How Beauvoir Talks Sex in English." *Contingent Loves: Simone de Beauvoir and Sexuality,* edited by Melanie C. Hawthorne, U of Virginia P, 2000, pp. 13–33.

Ihsane, Tabea, and Petra Sleeman. "Gender Agreement with Animate Nouns in French." *Romance Linguistics 2013: Selected Papers from the 43rd Linguistic Symposium on Romance Languages (LSRL), New York, 17–19 April, 2013,* edited by Christina Tortora et al., John Benjamins, 2016, pp. 159–176, https://doi.org/10.1075/rllt.9. Romance Languages and Linguistic Theory 9.

Vivien, Renée. *La dame à la louve.* Translated by Karla Jay and Yvonne M. Klein, Gay Presses of New York, 1983.

Renée Vivien

The Woman with the Wolf

The Woman with the Wolf

Told by M. Pierre Lenoir, 69 Rue des Dames[1]

I don't know why I undertook to court that woman. She wasn't beautiful, or pretty, or even nice. As for myself (and I can say this without conceit, dear ladies), there are those who have not been indifferent to me. It's not that Nature has endowed me so very extraordinarily, either physically or morally, but quite simply, if I may say so, that I have been very fortunate when it comes to the fair sex.[2] Oh, don't be alarmed: I'm not going to inflict on you some egocentric recital of my conquests. I'm a modest man. In any case, my story doesn't concern me at all this time. It has to do with a particular woman, or, to be more precise, a young lady, this Englishwoman, whose strange face pleased me in a passing moment.

1. *Noir* means "black," which for Vivien's readers might have had connotations of wickedness, while his address on the Rue des Dames ("Lady Street") is all too appropriate.

2. The French text simply refers to "le sexe" ("the sex"), which is understood to mean "the female sex." The locution underscores the fact that being male is the unmarked term in the male/female binary; it passes unremarked, whereas femaleness carries the mark of sex or gender: it is *the* sex.

She was an odd one. As I approached her for the first time, a great beast lay sleeping in the trailing folds of her skirt. On my lips were those amiable and banal remarks that ease relations among strangers. In any case, the words mean nothing; it's how you say them that counts. . . .

But the great beast, raising its muzzle, growled in a very sinister way, just as I approached the interesting stranger.

I took a step back in spite of myself.

"That's quite a vicious dog you have there, miss," I observed.

"She's a wolf," she replied, with a certain dryness of tone.[3] "And since she occasionally takes dislikes that are

3. This is the point in the French text where the sex and species of the companion animal becomes clear to Pierre. Until now, he has referred to the animal as "une bête," the French cognate word for "beast" and a feminine noun—which does not presuppose that the animal is biologically feminine—or as "un chien" ("a dog"), which also leaves the question open, as the generic masculine noun is the "universal" male that includes both sexes. It is only when the woman uses the word *louve*, the feminine form of the generic *loup* (from the Latin *lupus*), that the wolf's sex is specified in an unmistakable way. There are many symbolic associations with wolves, not least the image of the "lone wolf" outcast, but France also has a widespread tradition concerning a folkloric figure known as the *meneur de loups*, or leader of the wolf pack. This person is traditionally a wild or backwoods man with an almost supernatural hold over wolves (he is sometimes represented as a magician or even a werewolf). One popular fictional example can be found in Alexandre Dumas's *Le meneur de loups* (an English translation appeared in 1904, the same year as *La dame à la louve*), but there are

as violent as they are inexplicable, I believe you would do well to back off a little."

With one stern word, she hushed the wolf: "Helga!"

I beat my retreat, mildly humiliated. It was a stupid business, you must admit. Fear is foreign to me, but I hate ridicule. The incident bothered me even more since I thought I had detected a sympathetic glimmer in the young lady's eye. There was no doubt that I had pleased her somewhat. She must have been as annoyed as I was at this regrettable interference. What a pity! The conversation had seemed so promising to begin with. . . .

I don't know why that frightful animal later ceased its demonstrations of hostility. I was able to approach its mistress without fear. I've never seen such a strange face. Underneath her heavy blond hair, which was at once fiery and colorless, like burning ashes, glimmered the faint gray pallor of her complexion. Her emaciated body had the fine and fragile delicacy of a lovely skeleton.[4] (In Paris, we all have something of the artist in us,

---

many others. Here, the popular superstition merges with the fin de siècle image of the femme fatale to produce a terrifying image of female power combined with animal instincts and appetites. The French novelist Rachilde published a further twist on this theme in 1905 with her historical novel *Le meneur de louves*, in which it is the wolves themselves that are feminized. For more on French wolf mythology, see Jay M. Smith.

4. Anorexia is thought to be one of the causes (along with alcoholism and drug abuse) of Renée Vivien's early death in 1909.

you know.) This woman radiated an impression of tough and lonely pride, and of flight and frantic recoil. Her yellow eyes resembled those of her she-wolf. They bore the same expression of deceitful hostility. Her footsteps were so silent they became disturbing. No one ever made so little sound when they walked. She was dressed in a thick material that looked like a pelt. She wasn't beautiful, or pretty, or charming. But she was the only woman on board the ship.

And so I courted her. I observed the same rules that I had firmly established through long experience. She was clever enough to never let me see the deep pleasure my advances afforded her. She even knew how to preserve the habitual defiant expression of her yellow eyes. What a remarkable example of feminine wiles! The only result of that maneuver was to attract me to her even more violently. Lengthy resistance can have the effect on you of a pleasant surprise, and makes the victory even more brilliant. . . . You won't contradict me on this point, will you, gentlemen? We all share the same sentiments to some extent. Our common fellow-feeling is so complete that it almost makes conversation impossible. That's why I often flee the monotonous company of men; they are too much like me.

Admittedly, the Woman with the she-wolf attracted me. And what's more—must I admit it?—the enforced chastity of that floating jail exacerbated my tumultuous senses. She was a woman . . . and my suit, while still respectful, became more pressing every day. I piled up enflamed metaphors. I elegantly developed eloquent passages.

Observe to what lengths this woman carried her deceitfulness! Listening to me, she adopted an air of moonstruck distraction. You would have sworn she was only interested in the foaming wake that looked like steaming snow. (Women are by no means indifferent to poetic comparisons.) But I, who for so long had studied the psychology of the feminine face, understood that her heavy, lowered eyelids concealed the vacillating glimmers of love.

One day, when I was particularly bold, combining flattering gestures with delicate words, she turned to me with a she-wolf's bound.

"Go away," she commanded, with almost savage decisiveness. The wild animal teeth glinted strangely beneath lips drawn back in menace.

I smiled insouciantly. You have to be very patient with women, don't you? And never believe a single word they say?[5] When they order you to leave, you have to stay.

5. This story offers an early example of a woman's challenge to the widespread belief that "no means yes" when it comes to the seduction of women.

Really, gentlemen, I'm ashamed of offering you such tepid banalities.

The lady considered me with her large, yellow eyes.

"You're making a mistake with me. You are throwing yourself stupidly against my unassailable contempt. I can neither hate nor love. I've never met another human being worthy of my hatred. Hatred is more patient and enduring than love, and it requires a great adversary."

She caressed Helga's heavy head. The wolf looked at her with the deep eyes of a woman.

"As for love, I know as little about that as you know about the art of hiding men's inherent fatuousness, an art that is considered elementary among Anglo-Saxons. If I had been born a man, I might have loved a woman. For women have the qualities I value: loyalty in passion and the ability to put oneself aside in affection. For the most part, women are simple and sincere. They give of themselves without restriction and without counting the cost. Their patience is as inexhaustible as their kindness. They know how to forgive. They know how to wait. They possess that higher form of chastity: constancy."[6]

6. This speech by the Woman sums up some of the attitudes held by Vivien and her feminist contemporaries about women: they are not simply equal to men; they are better because more moral. This was

I don't lack finesse, and I don't have to have everything spelled out for me. I smiled meaningfully in response to this explosion of enthusiasm. She glanced at me with a distracted look that got my drift.

"Oh, you are making a strange mistake. I have come across women who are noble in spirit and in heart. But I have never attached myself to them. Their gentleness even set them at distance from me. My spirit wasn't lofty enough to keep patience with their excessive candor and devotion."

She was beginning to bore me with her pretentious speeches. A prude and a bluestocking as well as a flirt! . . . But she was the only woman on board. And besides she was only flaunting her superior airs in order to make her imminent capitulation more precious.

"I have affection only for Helga. And Helga knows it. As for you, you are no doubt a nice enough young man, but you can have no idea how much I despise you."

By arousing my pride, she meant to enflame my desire. And she was succeeding, the little imp! I was red with anger and lust.

"Men who crowd around women, any women, are like dogs sniffing around bitches."

---

one of the arguments advanced by women's suffrage movements at the time.

She gave me one of her long, yellow looks.

"I've breathed the forest air for so long, air vibrant with snow, I've mingled with such vast deserts of whiteness, that my spirit is partly that of a fleeting she-wolf."

The woman was finally starting to frighten me. She noticed it, and changed her tone.

"I have a love for clarity and freshness," she continued with a little laugh. "So, the vulgarity of men repels me like the reek of garlic, and their dirtiness repulses me like a gust of air from a sewer. Man," she insisted, "is only really at home in a brothel. He only loves courtesans. For he rediscovers in them his own rapacity, his own lack of emotional intelligence, his brutal cruelty. He lives only for self-interest or debauchery. Morally, he disgusts me; physically, he repulses me. . . . I've seen men kissing women on the lips while groping them obscenely. The sight of a gorilla wouldn't be more repellent."

She paused for a minute.

"It's only thanks to a miracle that the most austere legislator escapes the unfortunate consequences of the carnal promiscuity that is strewn across his youth. I can't understand how even the least sensitive woman can submit to your filthy kisses without gagging. Indeed, my virgin's contempt is equal in disgust to the courtesan's nausea."

Decidedly, I thought, she's exaggerating her part, though she understands it very well. She's exaggerating.

(If we were among ourselves, gentlemen, I would tell you that I have not always disdained the public houses[7] and that I have often picked up pitiful hookers on the street.[8] That doesn't stop Parisian women being more welcoming than that Holy Hands-Off.[9] I don't mean to be smug, but one should know one's worth.)

---

7. A public house in this sense is a brothel. It should not be confused with the British sense of a public house, or pub, as a place to consume alcohol.

8. There were several classes of prostitutes in French society at the turn of the century. The elite were the courtesans (or *grandes horizontales*) who provided escort services for the nobility in return for a lavish lifestyle. Renée Vivien knew some of these personally. For example, just before she met Natalie Barney, the latter had had a well-publicized affair with one of the most famous, Liane de Pougy, who recorded the liaison in a roman à clef, *Idylle saphique* (*Sapphic Idyll*). Prostitutes who worked in a "house" (a *maison close*) had the advantage of having a roof over their head, a community, and often both medical attention and police protection (although they could not count on long-term job security or retirement benefits). Prostitutes who worked in the streets, nicknamed *grues*, or "cranes" (because, like the bird, they often stood on one leg while waiting long hours), were at the bottom of the scale. There was a further distinction between women who worked for pimps and those who tried to go it alone (*les insoumises*). The latter had even less protection from exploitation by pimps, cheating or abuse from clients, harassment by police, and extortion, and had little control over working conditions. See Laure Adler and Luc Sante, especially chapter 7, "Le Business" (111–34).

9. The French word here, *sainte-nitouche*, puns on the idea of touching (*n'y touche*) to convey the idea of excessive virtue linked to religious scruples.

Deeming that the conversation had gone on long enough, I took my dignified leave of the Woman with the Wolf. Treacherous Helga followed me with her long, yellow gaze.

. . . Towering clouds were piling up on the horizon. Beneath them, a streak of dull blue-green sky wound like a moat. I felt as though I were being crushed between stone walls. . . .

The wind was picking up. . . .

I was seized with seasickness. . . . I do beg your pardon for such an inelegant detail, dear ladies. . . . I was horribly indisposed. . . . I finally fell asleep around midnight, feeling more pitiful than words can say.

Around two o'clock in the morning, I was awakened by a sinister jolt, followed by an even more sinister grinding sound. . . . The shadows breathed an inexpressible terror. I realized that the ship had struck a reef.[10]

10. The infamous sinking of the *Titanic* ocean liner after it struck an iceberg would not occur until 1912, three years after Vivien's death, but disasters at sea were not unknown in her own time. On 4 July 1898, for example, the French packet boat *La Bourgogne* collided with the British ship *Cromartyshire* not far from Halifax, Nova Scotia, in a thick fog, destroying half of the *Bourgogne*'s lifeboats in the process. In 1886, the *Bourgogne* had set a speed record for crossing the Atlantic, but this reputation proved to be its downfall: at the time of the accident, it was later determined, the ship was traveling at full speed despite the limited visibility. Most of the passengers were still in bed at the time of the collision, roughly 5:00 a.m. (which is perhaps why almost none in first class survived), and the ship sank, taking 549 lives in the process.

For the first time in my life, I neglected my appearance. I threw on some clothes and appeared on the deck.

A confused crowd of half-naked men was already swarming about. . . . They were rapidly launching the lifeboats.

When I saw those hairy arms and those shaggy chests, I couldn't help remembering, not without a smile, the remark made by the Woman with the Wolf: *"The sight of a gorilla would not be more repulsive. . . ."*

I don't know why, but this futile memory mocked me in the midst of this common danger.

The waves looked like monstrous volcanoes wreathed in white smoke. Or, to be more exact, they resembled nothing at all. They were themselves—magnificent, terrible, deadly. . . . The wind blew over this oversized wrath and increased it further. The salt bit at my eyes. I shivered in the spray as though in a cold drizzle. And the crashing of the waves blotted out all thought in me.

At first the *Cromartyshire* did not realize what had happened, but once the fog began to lift (at around 5:30), it began to render assistance. Of the 173 survivors of the disaster, fewer than 70 were passengers (out of 506); the remainder were crew members (over 100 survivors out of a crew of 220). Sensationalist newspaper accounts made much of this, reporting that the crew not only failed to help passengers escape but even at times assaulted them, so that the crew members who later made it to New York needed police protection from the outraged public who greeted them.

The Woman with the Wolf was as calm as ever. As for myself, I was fainting from terror. I saw Death standing in front of me. I could almost touch Her. In a dazed sort of way, I fingered my forehead, where I could feel the bones of my skull bulging frightfully. The skeleton within me terrified me. Like an idiot, I started to cry. . . .

I would be black and blue flesh, more swollen than a distended wineskin. This way and that, the sharks would snap at one of my dismembered limbs. And when I had fallen to the bottom of the sea, the crabs would scuttle sideways along my rotted corpse and gluttonously eat their fill. . . .

The wind blew over the waters. . . .

I relived my past. I repented for my idiotic life, my spoiled life, my lost life. I tried to remember one act of kindness I had performed casually or without calculation. Had I ever been good for anything, useful to anyone? And my obscured conscience shrieked inside me, as horrifying as a mute who has miraculously recovered his speech:

"No!"

The wind blew over the waters. . . .

I dimly remembered the sacred words that exhorted repentance and that promised, even at the hour of death, salvation to the contrite sinner. I strove to retrieve from my memory, drier now than an empty goblet, a few words of prayer. . . . And carnal thoughts rose to torment me, like little red imps. I relived the beds soiled by chance companions. I heard once more their stupidly obscene cries. I re-experienced the loveless embraces. A horror of Pleasure overwhelmed me. . . .

In the face of my terror at the Mysterious Immensity, nothing survived in me save the rutting instinct, stronger in some than the instinct for self-preservation. It was Life, the ugliness and grossness of Life, that was screaming inside me a ferocious protest against Annihilation.

The wind blew over the waters. . . .

One has peculiar ideas at times like that, all the same. . . . Here I was, a very decent lad, admired by all, except for a few who were jealous of me, and even loved by some. Here I was reproaching myself quite bitterly for an existence that was neither better nor worse than anyone else's. I must have succumbed to a moment of madness. We were all a little mad, in any event. . . .

The Woman with the Wolf, completely calm, looked out at the white waves. . . . Oh! They were whiter than the snow at twilight! And, seated on her haunches, Helga howled like a dog. She howled pitifully, like a dog baying at the moon. . . . She understood.

I don't know why her howling chilled me even more than the noise of the wind and the waves. . . . She howled at death, that damned wolf-devil. I wanted to knock her senseless to shut her up and I looked for a plank, a spar, an iron bar, anything just to beat her to the deck. . . . I found nothing. . . .

The lifeboat was at last ready to leave. The men leapt frantically toward salvation. Only the Woman with the Wolf didn't move at all.

"Get on board," I shouted at her as I took my turn to climb into the boat.

She came toward the boat without haste, followed by Helga.

"Mademoiselle," said the lieutenant, who was commanding us as well as he could, "we can't take that animal with us. There isn't enough room for all the people."

"In that case, I'll stay," she said, stepping back. . . .

The terror-stricken men rushed forward with incoherent cries. We had to let her stay behind.[11]

---

11. In cases of disaster, the saying "Women and children first" would normally be a guiding principle in theory. In this instance, we know that there are no children on board, and there is only one woman, but chivalry would dictate that concern for her safety should have been one of the men's first thoughts. The self-interested behavior of the men on Pierre's ship belies such chivalry, however. In the case of the *Bourgogne* shipwreck (see note above), none of the children on board survived, and only one woman survived out of some 300, but in that instance, concern about the gender ratio of survivors was eclipsed by the scandal surrounding the ratio of crew members to passengers. Outrage over men's failure to protect women was stoked, however, by a domestic, land-based catastrophe that took place the same year as the sinking of the *Bourgogne*. Vivien's readers in fin de siècle Paris may well have recalled the recent terrible fire at the Bazar de la Charité in 1897,

Personally, I couldn't really make a fool of myself. And furthermore, she had been so insolent to me. You understand that, gentlemen, don't you? You wouldn't have acted any differently from me.

In the end I was saved, or just about. Dawn broke, and my God, what a dawn! There was a shiver of chilling light, a gray stupor, a larval swarm of persons and things in a dusky confusion of limbs. . . .

And we saw the blue outline of land in the distance. . . .

Oh, what joy and comfort to see the sure and welcoming land! . . . Since this horrible experience, I have made only one journey by sea, and that was to return here. I won't ever make another, you may be sure!

I must not be too much of an egotist, dear ladies. In the midst of the unspeakable certainty with which I struggled, and though I had barely escaped Destruction, I still had the courage to concern myself with the fate

when a temporary wooden structure built to house an annual charity event patronized by the aristocracy suddenly went up in flames. The event was a shock to the public, not only because of the high number of deaths from the elite classes but also because so many men had saved themselves without helping women and children escape the blaze. The fire claimed 125 victims, of whom 120 were women. Of the five male victims, two were elderly men and two were children (aged four and eleven). The flower of French manhood escaped unscathed, and stories in the press circulated about men who had even used their canes to knock women aside in order to escape (see Datta). Among other things, the event challenged the argument that women were protected by men and therefore did not need social and political rights.

of my companions in misfortune. The second lifeboat had been swamped by the assault of too many madmen. With horror, I saw it sink. . . . The Woman with the Wolf had taken refuge on a broken mast, along with her obedient animal. . . . I was quite sure that if the strength and endurance of this woman did not betray her, she would be saved. I hoped so, with all my heart. . . . But there was the cold, the sluggishness and fragility of her improvised raft, which lacked sails and rudder, her fatigue, her feminine weakness!

They were a short distance from land when the Woman, exhausted, turned toward Helga, as if to say, "I'm finished. . . ."

And then a most mournful and solemn thing occurred. The she-wolf, *who had understood*, hurled her howl of despair toward the nearby yet unattainable shore. . . . Then, drawing herself upright, she put her two forepaws on her mistress's shoulders, who in turn embraced her. . . . Together, they both disappeared beneath the waves. . . .

Sniggering Thirst

Told by Jim Nicholls

"What a peculiar sunset!" I said to Polly.

We were traveling on our mules, which were weighed down by the heat and by weariness.

"Idiot!" growled my companion. "Can't you see that the light is coming from the east?"

"That would be dawn, then. I must be drunk, except I haven't had a drink all day."

The sleepy gait of our mules rocked me gently in my dreams.

We were in the middle of the open prairie. . . . Before us was a desert of pale grass. Behind us lay an ocean of pale grass. All around us prowled Thirst. I could see its parched lips moving. I could hear its feverish mutterings. Polly, that bitch with hair like straw, saw nothing, which didn't surprise me at all. Polly couldn't see anything beyond the end of her nose reddened by the fresh air and sun.

I turned in my saddle and pulled sharply on the reins.

"Why are you stopping?" Polly asked me.

"I'm looking at Thirst.[1] Its robes are as gray as the dry grass down there. It's making a face. It's sniggering. The contortions of its carcass make me afraid. It's certainly ugly enough, is Thirst."

Polly shrugged her heavy shoulders heavily.

"You're crazy, Jim. Only fools like you have nightmares in broad daylight."

I would cheerfully have slapped or kicked her to shut her up, but repeated painful experiences had convinced me that Polly was far stronger than me. All I had over her was some vague mental superiority. And even so, my companion's good sense had often gotten me out of a tight spot, something that my own soft-headed drifting could never have done.

I'd had some education, it's true, but what good is an education on the prairies? A good revolver is worth a lot more there.

Polly's hair flamed implacably in the light. I suddenly felt like scalping her, the way my friends and adversaries the Indians do, to spatter that blond mop of hair with

---

1. The noun *soif* ("thirst") is grammatically feminine in French, so that in the French text, whenever Jim refers to it, he uses feminine pronouns (there is no neuter option). These have been translated as "it" and "its," but the reader should keep in mind this underlying personification of thirst as a feminine predator throughout the story. See the note on the translation for more on how grammatical gender influences such figurative thinking.

blood.[2] Why? I don't know. That's just the sort of idea that comes over you like that on the prairies.

I looked at her cheeks, browned like two baked apples. I don't know why I remembered just at that particular moment a pale, thin face I had once loved. I summoned up a shady cottage, the coolness of closed shutters, and the beautiful eyelids of a woman reading. How charming she was with her lids lowered like that! I adored the shadow of her eyelashes on her pale cheeks. Ah! . . .

In those days, I knew nothing at all about being a prairie rider. I hadn't yet met the bitch with the hair like straw.

Why did I leave that shady cottage and the green light that filtered through the closed shutters? I don't know.

Any more than I know if that strange little girl who read for those long hours is dead or alive. I think she must be dead because sometimes I feel such an emptiness in my heart!

But I'm not sure of anything.

It makes your thoughts a bit disturbed when you see the specter of Thirst prowling round you on the prairie.

2. It may be useful to consider the experience of Vivien's mother growing up in the "frontier" town of Jackson, Michigan, where a child was abducted by Indians (or so it was claimed in the press) in 1837. See Hawthorne, "Des antécédents américains."

I chose Polly, whom I detest, as my traveling companion, or rather, she chose me. I'll end up killing her one of these days. That I know. I hate her because she is so disgustingly healthy, whereas I'm such a feverish weakling. She's tougher and more solid than a man. She could send me rolling six feet with just the flick of a wrist. But she's a gentle giant, when she hasn't had too much to drink. She does like to get drunk, though. Maybe she, too, is afraid of Thirst, who's lying in wait for both of us.

I chanced a remark along the way.

"There's going to be a storm before long, Polly, light of my life."

"Idiot!" she breathed with conviction. "Leave me alone. You only ever say stupid things. Of course there'll be a storm before long. It looks like it and it smells like it, and I don't like chatter for the sake of it."

"Oh, my sweet thing, your wisdom is just as benevolent as it is profound."

She didn't bother to answer me. One of these days, I'm going to end up killing her for sure. I won't have the strength to strangle her, but I'll shoot her in the back with a single revolver shot. That way, it'll all be over with and I won't have to think about her any more. Maybe Thirst will stop following me, if I give it some blood to drink. Who knows?

. . . The unnatural dawn grew more intense. . . . We came to a halt, as it was evening. Polly poured me a drop of liquor from her well-rounded flask. I drank to her early death. All of a sudden, the bitch stopped drinking.

That surprised me a bit. Only something really unusual could distract Polly from the extreme satisfaction to be had in her favorite drink.

"What's the matter with you?" I asked, with affectionate interest.

Polly hates to waste a word, indeed. I'll give her that. Her long journeys under the sun have made her taciturn. She really is the perfect companion for a man of the prairies. . . . She simply pointed to some ashes mixed with gray grass.

I understood what she was thinking. Instinctively, my eyes turned toward the peculiar dawn that was reddening the east. But a little rise got in the way of my seeing what was happening over there.

Polly spat out a muffled curse. . . . My knees buckled beneath me. She looked me scornfully up and down, and without saying a word, she left me and set off up the hill.

I followed her, because I feared being left behind more than I detested her company.

When we reached the top of the rise, we gasped. . . .

From north to south, the horizon was one big, blazing inferno.

A prairie fire!

A fiery wind that rushes over you with the speed of a simoom or a sirocco, that sweeps over that desert of dry grass in the blink of an eye.[3] And nothing in its way to stop it!

I was shaking like a sick man dying of fever. . . . But Polly wasn't the least afraid.

For a minute, I forgot my own terror in my fury that she wasn't shaking with fear. Her terror would almost have calmed my own horror. But she's brave, much braver than I ever am. She didn't turn pale, because nothing, not a single thing, not even death or the trumpet of the Last Judgment, could make her blanch. . . . In any case, she has a particularly ruddy complexion. As for me, I was as yellow as a gold coin.

We returned as quickly as possible toward our improvised camp, where we had left our mules grazing; fear was making them skittish.

The evening breeze was pushing that firestorm in our direction.

3. The simoom (from Arabic) is a dry, dusty wind that blows in the deserts of the Middle East, while the sirocco is a Mediterranean wind that blows from the Sahara. Both can be strong and life-threatening.

I'm not afraid of death, but pain horrifies me. The prospect of being roasted alive was the height of torture to me. Even Polly herself looked grim, though her nerves were tougher than ox tendon.

. . . Roasted alive on the prairie! . . .

The fire sprang toward us like an enormous flash of lightning. I was amazed at how quickly it spread. A few more minutes and the two of us would be charcoal. A few more minutes and . . .

. . . This torrent of flame was beautiful all the same. It was more beautiful than the sun. I've never seen anything more magnificent. . . . It was so marvelously splendid that I fell to my knees and stretched both hands out to the Fire, laughing like a baby or an idiot.

I repeat, it was as terrible as it was superb, and that drove me almost crazy. The sight was too beautiful for human eyes. God alone could look directly at such a conflagration without dying or going mad.

But Polly, who has about as much soul as my mules, didn't understand any of this, and looked without seeing. Nothing astonishes her, and nothing compels her admiration. . . .

I hated her for not being afraid. Oh, how I hated her! . . . I hate her ferociously, because she's stronger and more valiant than me. . . . I hate her the way a woman loathes the man who dominates her. One of these days,

I'll wind up killing her for sure, if only for the sheer pleasure of conquering her. . . .

"Let's not waste any time," said Polly resolutely. She spoke in her usual everyday voice, neither raising it nor lowering it by so much as half a tone. (Oh, how I hated her for being so calm!) She squatted down and, in the blink of an eye, set fire to the grass in front of her.

I thought for a second that she had gone mad, too. I whooped with joy, like an avenging Indian.

She wasn't bothered at all. She was used to my bizarre moods. She had too much contempt for me to be afraid of me.

"Fire fights fire, Jim."

We drew back. Our fire burned steadily, like a nice fire in a peaceful home. The other fire, fed by the thousands of acres of grass it had consumed, advanced like an ocean wave made of light and noise.

. . . I shut my eyes, drunk with the smoke. . . . When I opened them again, two hours later, everything around us was black. These were the ruins of the blaze. The furnace had miraculously put itself out.

Fire had vanquished Fire.

Polly had planted herself proudly in front of me, hands on hips. What made me furious was that she had not been the least afraid for a single second.

Any more than she'll be afraid on the day I kill her, because she's not afraid of death. She's not afraid of God, either. . . .

She was looking at me without flinching.

"What a coward you are!" she said, disdainfully.

Prince Charming

Told by Gesa Karoly[1]

I promised you, my curious little girl, to tell you the true story of Sarolta Andrassy. You knew her, didn't you? You remember her black hair with blue and red highlights, and her eyes like a lover's, begging and melancholy.

Sarolta Andrassy lived in the country with her old mother. For neighbors, she had the Szecheny family, who had just left Budapest forever.[2] Really, they were a

---

1. The story is set in Hungary and told by a Hungarian. It is usual in Hungarian culture to state the family name before a person's given name, but it is difficult to tell whether Vivien does so here, since both Karoly and Gesa can be boys' first names. Karoly is the Hungarian cognate of Charles or Karl, but to those who don't know Hungarian, it may look like the traditionally feminine name Carole, thereby encoding gender confusion in the very source of the tale. The fact that Hungarian does not belong to a dominant European language group (such as the Romance or Germanic languages) and is opaque to many Europeans helps Vivien establish a sense of mystery in this story.

2. Budapest, as the capital of Hungary is now known, was originally two separate cities (Buda and Pest, or Pesth), one on each side of the Danube river, that grew together and merged. At the turn of the century, Hungary was part of a world superpower, the Austro-Hungarian Empire (which would be wiped off the map by World War I). Yet there was a persistent perception in western Europe that the eastern parts of the empire were more primitive and "backward" than the West (such as cosmopolitan Vienna, the capital of Austria).

bizarre family! It was easy to mistake Bela Szecheny for a little girl and his sister, Terka, for a little boy.[3] Curiously enough, Bela possessed all the feminine virtues, and Terka all the masculine faults. Bela's hair was a greenish blond; Terka's was a livelier, rather reddish blond. The brother and sister strangely resembled each other—and that's very rare among members of the same family, no matter what anyone says.

Bela's mother was not yet resigned to cutting off the beautiful blond curls of the little boy or to exchanging his graceful muslin or velvet skirts for vulgar pants.[4] She

---

For example, in Bram Stoker's *Dracula* of 1897, Jonathan Harker sets off from Vienna to travel to the Carpathian mountains in eastern Europe, and the further east he travels, the further back in time he seems to go. This establishes Transylvania as a credible place to be attacked by vampires, an ancient species that has evaded detection in the more "enlightened" West.

3. The name Bela, though commonly given to boys, invites readers to see it as a cognate of Bella, a word that means "beautiful" in Italian and was familiar as a name or nickname for girls.

4. It was common in Vivien's day to make little distinction in appearance between boys and girls in the early years of their lives. Until the age of about six or seven (the age varied), boys wore a garment that resembled a dress (easier for toilet training), and their hair remained uncut, growing into long curls. When the time came to put them in their first pair of pants, an event known in England and America as "breeching" (because *breeches* was another name for pants or trousers), they would also have their first haircut, and this was the signal that they were now "little men." At this point, their upbringing might be taken over by their father, they were often separated from their mother and her sphere of influence, and they might be sent away to school. This stage often marked a sad time for mothers, who felt they had

coddled him like a little girl. As for Terka, she grew taller and taller, like an unruly weed. . . . She lived outdoors, climbing trees, marauding, pillaging the kitchen gardens. She was unbearable and at war with everyone. She was neither a tender nor a communicative child. Bela, on the other hand, was gentleness itself. He showed his adoration for his mother by stroking and caressing her all the time. Terka loved no one, and no one loved her.

Sarolta came one day to visit the Szecheny family. Her loving eyes in her thin, pale face seemed imploring. She liked Bela a great deal, and they played together a long time. Looking wild, Terka prowled around them. When Sarolta spoke to her, she ran off.

She could have been pretty, this incomprehensible Terka. . . . But she was too tall for her age, too thin, too awkward, too ungainly, whereas Bela was so dainty and so sweet! . . .

Several months later, the Szecheny family left Hungary. Sarolta cried bitterly over losing her playmate. On the advice of the doctor, his mother had taken him to Nice, along with his recalcitrant little sister.[5] Bela had

"lost" their sons, which explains why Bela's mother was delaying this moment.

5. Nice was a common destination for those seeking a healthier climate. Anton Chekhov went there in 1898 when suffering from tu-

an extremely delicate chest, and was not very robust in general.

In her dreams, Sarolta always evoked the too frail and too pretty little boy whom she persisted in remembering. And she would say to herself, smiling at the blond fantasy, "If I must get married when I'm older, I would like to marry Bela."

Several years passed—oh, how slowly for the impatient Sarolta! Bela must have reached the age of twenty, and Terka seventeen. They were still on the Riviera. And Sarolta grieved through the long, joyless years, which were brightened only by the illusion of a dream.

One violet evening, she was dreaming by her window when her mother came to tell her that Bela had returned. . . .

Sarolta's heart sang as if it would burst. And, the next day, Bela came to her.

He was the same, and yet even more charming than before. Sarolta was happy that he had kept this feminine and gentle manner that had so pleased her. He was still the fragile child. . . . But now this child possessed an inexpressible grace. Sarolta searched in vain for the cause of this transformation that made him so attractive.

berculosis. Renée Vivien was also a frequent visitor to Nice (see Hawthorne, "Two Nice Girls").

His voice was musical and distant like the echo of the mountains. She admired everything about him, right down to his stone-gray English suit and his mauve necktie.[6]

Bela contemplated the young woman with different eyes, with strangely beautiful eyes, with eyes that weren't like the eyes of other men. . . .

"How thin he is!" observed Sarolta's mother after he had gone. "Poor thing, he must still be in delicate health."

Sarolta didn't answer. She closed her eyes so as to see Bela again under her closed eyelids. . . . He was so pretty, pretty, pretty! . . .

He returned the next day, and every day after that. He was the Prince Charming seen only in the pages of childhood fairy stories. She couldn't look him in the face without feeling ardently and langorously faint. . . . Her face changed according to the expression on the face she loved. Her heart beat according to the rhythm of that other heart. Her carefree and childish tenderness had turned into love.

Bela would turn pale as soon as she appeared, diaphanous in her white summer dress. Sometimes he looked

6. The color mauve was a relatively new invention and closely associated with decadence (see Garfield).

at her without speaking, like someone contemplating a perfect statue. Sometimes he took her hand. . . . His palm was so burning hot and dry that she thought she was touching the hand of an invalid. Indeed, at those times a little fever would flush Bela's cheeks.

One day she asked him for some news of the undisciplined Terka.

"She's still in Nice," he answered carelessly. And then they spoke of other things. Sarolta understood that Bela didn't love his sister at all. Which was not surprising, after all—a girl who was so taciturn and wild!

The inevitable happened. A few months later, Bela asked to marry her. He had just entered his twenty-first year. Sarolta's mother had no objection to the union.

Their engagement was unreal, as delicate as the white roses that Bela brought every day. Their vows were more fervent than poems; their very souls trembled on their lips. The nuptial dream unfolded in the deepest silence.

"Why," Sarolta would ask her fiancé, "are you worthier of being loved than other young men? Why do you have gentle ways that they don't? Where did you learn the divine words that they never say?"

The wedding ceremony took place in absolute privacy. The candles brightened the red highlights in Bela's blond hair. The smoke from the incense curled toward him, and the thunder of the organs exalted and glorified him.

For the first time since the beginning of the world, the Groom was as beautiful as the Bride.

They left for those blue shores where the desire of lovers runs out of patience. They were seen, a Divine Couple, with the eyelashes of one brushing the eyelids of the other. They were seen, lovingly and chastely intertwined, with her black hair spread over his blond hair. . . .

But this—oh, my curious little girl!—is where the story gets a little difficult to tell. . . . Several months later, the real Bela Szecheny appeared. . . . He was not Prince Charming, alas! He was only a handsome boy, nothing more.

He furiously sought the identity of the young usurper. . . . And he learned that the usurper in question was his own sister, Terka.[7]

. . . . Sarolta and Prince Charming have never returned to Hungary. They are hiding in the depths of a Venetian castle or of a Florentine mansion. And sometimes they are seen, as one sees a vision of ideal tenderness, lovingly and chastely intertwined.

7. As Mireille Rosello has noted, this story rewrites (from a feminist perspective) what folklorists refer to as the "bed trick" narrative, where one person secretly replaces another in a sexual encounter without the other partner seeming to notice (179n8). For other examples of the bed trick, see Wendy Doniger, *The Bedtrick* and *The Woman Who Pretended to Be Who She Was*.

The Sisters of Silence

I had heard tell, sometimes in terms of praise, sometimes in terms of contempt, of this lay monastery that was created out of the pain of one woman to shelter the pain of other women. Some maintained that it was a fraternal and holy place where the weariness of women could be tempered by meditation. Others saw in it nothing but the unhealthy whim of someone who had been led astray by grief.

I was resolved to see and learn for myself, and, one autumn day, I went to the secular convent.

The Superior greeted me with taciturn grace. Everything about her had a harmonious grayness—her hair and her eyes, and the melancholy folds of her cowl.

"May I enquire . . . ?" I began with awkward clumsiness.

"Do not ask me anything at all," interrupted the Gray Lady, not unkindly. "A question is a brutal violation of the right and duty of silence. Look and observe, learn for yourself, but never ask anything from one who is as weak and uncertain as you are."

. . . And so I lived and I learned in that strange lay monastery created out of the pain of one woman to shelter the pain of other women.

The convent appeared to be fading in the midst of an immense garden where only virginal white flowers grew, the blossoms of sterility and death. Only the youngest among the recluses were permitted to lavish on the plants and shrubbery the delicate care that is the usual responsibility of gardeners. For the gross hand of man, according to the law of the convent, could never be allowed to soil the flowers.

The most mystical of silences reigned throughout the convent. Those who were still tormented by the memory of the word[1] went on rare occasions to the "parlor,"[2] where they took up once again, for a few moments, the vain practice of human speech. Then they returned with a peaceful joy to the monastic Dream.

---

1. The French word here is *verbe*, which can be translated as "verb" but also as "language." The translation "word" reflects the echo in the original text of biblical passages such as "In the beginning was the Word" (*Bible*, John 1:1).

2. Vivien is drawing attention to the etymology of the word *parlor*, which would be more transparent in French than in English. The parlor is often thought of as merely a space for social interactions of all sorts, but since it is derived from the verb for talking (*parler*), in the convent the designation of the room can be taken literally.

The rites of the house of isolation and repose took place by the sad light of the setting sun. Young women with flowing hair murmured verse or intoned their chants. A few fervent solitary souls wandered through the galleries, their gaze held captive by the splendor of the paintings and statues. Others gathered pale flowers from the greenhouses and the gardens or lingered to contemplate the vastness of the twilight and of the sea.

Like an eagle's nest, the pious residence hugged the rocks. Passersby feared the violence of its scent. Once, long ago, the inexorable waft of orange blossom had brought about the death of a virgin.

At the foot of the monastery, the blue abyss glistened, exercising even greater attraction than the waves of the Mediterranean. The windows were wide, and, since they were always wide open to the sea, they encompassed the entire glorious curve of the Rainbow. When the organ thundered and flashed, when the violins sobbed out all their divine anguish, the waves mingled their single-toned rhythm with those eternal songs.

The youngest Sister appeared to me like the incarnation of my most beautiful thought. Her robe was the same violet color as the evening. This woman reminded me of the fragility of mother-of-pearl and the lofty sadness of the black swans who leave a darkness in their wake.[3] In response to my silence, she murmured:

"In these shadows, I have not sought peace, like some Exile knocking at the door of the monastery, but the Infinite."

And I saw that hers was the divine face of Solitude.

3. The black swan has a special place in Vivien's imagination, where it seems to embody the avian equivalent of a black sheep. Figuratively speaking, the black sheep is the misfit in a family, one who is stigmatized and ostracized.

The Cruelty of Jewels

Told by Giuseppe Bianchini

Truly, Madonna Gemma, you are aptly named. You are the dazzling and impervious sister of jewels. . . . I love those aquamarines that are the color of your eyes. Aquamarines are the most beautiful of all gems: they have the cold transparency of wintry waves.[1]

How you love the precious stones that adorn you, oh, my most beautiful Lady! Their dormant life blends with your breath and the steady beating of your arteries. Ah, these pearls that embrace your voluptuous and cruel neck! Ah, the depths of those emeralds and the thrill of these opals!

Do you recall why, once upon a time, I lost myself in parchments and crucibles for so many long months? I wanted to discover the Philosopher's Stone for you.[2] I

1. The name Gemma, which echoes the theme of precious stones (*pierres précieuses*) in its evocation of the word *gem* works in both French (*une gemme*) and English. *Madonna* here is an Italian form of address ("my lady"), not a religious reference.

2. The philosopher's stone would reputedly turn ordinary metals into gold and was sought (unsuccessfully) by alchemists. The crucible was used in the ancient practice of alchemy.

wanted gold, gold, gold, a stream of gold to pour into your lap. Your body would have bent under the weight of your adornments. The splendor of your necklaces and your rings would have humiliated the Dogaressa.[3] The prow of your gondola would have blinded people with its rubies, leaving the reflection of an autumn sun on the water. . . .

. . . How you sparkle in the shadows! . . . Turn your eyes of beryl away from me. Madonna, your implacable soul smiles through your eyes. . . .

There are bizarre and awful men who are enchanted by the physical suffering of others.[4] The cries and contortions of the tortured sharpen their jaded senses. . . . You are just like them, you who are repulsed by the ugliness of physical suffering and by the barbarism of spilt blood. Your joy is to rekindle the agony that slumbers in the soul. The vision of my fear and suffering burns through my words. That is why you listen to me re-

---

3. The Republic of Venice was governed by an elected leader, the doge, who was crowned and treated like royalty. A dogaressa is the wife of a doge.

4. The concept of sadism—taking sexual pleasure in the pain of others—was not new in Vivien's time (it was named for the eighteenth-century marquis de Sade), but the literary movement of decadence at the end of the nineteenth century had stimulated renewed interest in various forms of sexual perversion.

counting them with such a bright smile. . . . You are pitiless, Madonna Gemma. But you are so beautiful that I will obey you.

My laborious nights as an alchemist created this strange mood in me, which both pleases and displeases you. Ah, those labor-filled nights! I dimly sensed that someone was spying on my secret studies. You know that as well as I do, perhaps better. Someone whose invisible eyes watched me work denounced me to the Inquisition. I was accused of black magic. By whom? Perhaps you know, Madonna. Perhaps you know that, because of this denunciation, seven years ago I was walled up in a shadowy prison.

How can I possibly convey the horrors of that dungeon that never saw the dawn? . . . But my most vivid torture was to see my patient research interrupted at the very moment when I was about to discover the Philosopher's Stone. A few hours more, and I would have been the master of all the gold and all the gems in the universe.

For a long time I dreamed with the intolerable obsession of the damned. I saw you in a flash of jewels. I loved you with an inexpressible hatred. With a wave of your hand you would point out the iron door, the bars on the window, and the locks. During the night, my tortures were more diabolical than ever. Fever and Dementia carried me off like a sirocco. . . .[5] I sank in an ocean of shadows.

And in order to be reunited with you—do not tremble so much, my dazzling Mistress—in order to find you again and to torture you expertly with infinite caresses of cruelty, I wanted to escape from my shadowy prison.

. . . On an evening that was greener than an April river, the jailer entered, with a creak of rusted iron. He looked at me with amused scorn. I had always acted as meekly as a baby mule. I was as tearfully obedient as a battered child.

He asked me whether my fever had subsided at all. I answered with a groan, but along with my wailing I mixed some protestations of gratitude for the interest he was expressing in me.

He headed for the door after some stupid words of encouragement. With a furious leap, I grabbed him from behind and bit him ferociously on the neck. It was such a big shock that he fell backward without uttering a cry. With one hand I gagged him with some straw from my cell. Then, seizing the bunch of heavy keys that hung from his belt, I vigorously battered him to death.

---

5. The sirocco is a Mediterranean wind that travels north from the Sahara desert to Italy, often carrying sand, and associated with illness.

He took a long time to die, and more than once I nearly lost patience before I finally saw a river of blood that streamed with the debris of his brains.

The hideousness of this sight disgusted me a bit, but this man was too stupid for me to waste much time regretting his loss. I stripped him, hid my own bloody clothes under the ample cloak he always wore, and crossed the dark corridors.

. . . The harsh voice of a drunken woman brought me up short in a cold sweat and trembling more than a Romagnol peasant[6] brought down by malaria.

"Hurry up, Beppo! The soup's steaming on the table."

In one of those insights brought on by extreme terror, I understood that the wife of the late jailer was going to give me away.

I turned around. In a flash I took in the whole woman. First, I noticed that she was abominably drunk. Her breasts hung down on her fat stomach like two empty wineskins, as though she were pregnant. In the semi-darkness, her nose glowed like a setting sun. On her fat lips, the musty smell of cheap wine was growing increasingly sharp. Her badly dyed hair was red in patches. Heavy gold rings weighed down her pendulous ears,

6. "Romagnol" refers to an inhabitant of Italian region of Emilia-Romagna.

which were more accustomed to the bellowing of slaughtered animals than to serenades. She was staggering, and from her throat escaped some sour belches.

What struck me most was the coarse coquetry of her clothes. Her scarlet skirt was blazing like a bonfire; her bodice, an aggressive yellow, rang out like the trumpets of victory. Several strands of coral coiled around her short, fat neck, which would be so easy to squeeze between murderous hands. . . . Necks like that are asking to be strangled, just as certain long, pale frailties are asking to be raped.

A plan, as unformulated as instinct, sprang from my delirious brain. . . . I fell at the knees of the enormous peasant woman.

"Madonna," I sighed with grandiloquence, like a sentimental clown, "forgive this ruse on the part of a too fervent worshipper that has brought him the good fortune of being allowed to enter your presence."

She studied me with her gaping snout, her mind scrambled by the tavern wines.

"Fear not, oh beautiful redhead, incarnation of autumn's setting sun! I locked your husband in an empty cell, after I roughed him up a bit. I stuffed straw in his mouth, like you do with the donkeys he so takes after. Silenced like that, he will not be able to interrupt our passionate conversation."

I courageously embraced her kneecaps. Her unsteady pupils dilated with astonishment and terror.

A rapid thought crossed my mind. At the moment they arrested me, I had just set a delicate ring meant for you. Two sirens, their scales and tangled hair carved in gold that had turned green, were holding in their cupped arms an aquamarine as beautiful as a drop of frozen sea water. I had succeeded in concealing this gem. I offered it to this creature, whose mammaries shook with a convulsive trembling.

"I forged this ring for you, oh shining light of my dreams!"

A smile of thoughtless bliss swelled the lips of the heavy sot.

"Last night, when the first stars made the dead water shimmer with illusory life, I hid in the shadows, and I sang impassioned canzoni for you."

"I remember," sighed the drunkard, swooning with pleasure, as if a hand had skillfully tickled her. "Oh! Yes, I do remember. I clearly heard a beautiful bass voice that rose so lovingly toward me. But I thought I recognized the tone of that gondolier who has been courting my daughter Guiseppina for the last three months."

"When dawn opened like a rose, I was still under your window, Madonna. I was composing fervent litanies in your honor, as if for the Santissima Vergine. . . .[7] You are the flame of Venice, the mirage of the setting sun, the smile of darkened waves. . . . And in my dreams I named you Violante."

"My name is Onesta," interrupted the dreadful old hag, while complacently stroking her overflowing mammaries.

"I'll confess everything, Onesta mia. I am a great lord whose palace doors will open wide for you in triumph. Your feet, like those of a wandering child, will be reflected in marble of almost diaphanous purity—a wave carrying snow. Listen, Onesta. A dress of silver fabric gleaming with pearls will cover the melodious curve of your hips. Aquamarines married to moonstones will give you the appearance of starlight on the sea. Two ladies-in-waiting will carry the royal weight of your train, laden with precious metal and jewels. And two amorous pages, kneeling in front of your throne, will take turns singing tender verses that I will dictate to them. I shall not offer you flowers, my enchantress, for your eyes must not know the sadness of the death throes of a rose. You shall contemplate only the everlasting beauty of opals and emeralds. And into your onyx cup I will pour

7. The Santissima Vergine is "the most holy virgin" in Italian.

wines as glorious as victories, as sweet as poison, and as vehement as kisses. . . ."

Hearing me mention wine, my reeling conquest drooled with joy. A light flitted across her haggard eyes.

"Wine!" she sighed.

"Let me lead you away, Onesta," I beseeched her. "Follow me to love's palace where the bridal bed is already prepared. I am a magician, and I know special caresses learned from perverse archangels."

I stopped to savor the effect produced by my eloquence. Then, knowing that women prefer concrete gestures to the most lavish promises, I leaned toward her. I brushed Onesta's red neck with my breath made bland by the mean prison diet. . . . Seeing the encouraging shudders of all this chianti-sodden flesh, I dared to execute some further expert moves, which produced a fresh round of belches. I continued, insinuating and enticing:

"I will teach you the red-hot spice of love bites. . . . I will teach you the insidious insistence of lips and the tenacity of a slow hand. . . . No doubt your boorish husband has left you in the dark about these things. . . ."

Abruptly, I dropped all the formalities. "Come on, Onesta! . . ."

She fixed her stunned eyes on me.

"Indeed, you have the words and manners of a great lord," she stammered, "but I can't leave my husband and children for you."

"Will your husband be able to adorn your feminine splendor as magnificently as I can? Will he know how to match precious stones to the highlights of your eyes? What's more, you are too graceful to be just a mother, Onesta."

"Perhaps that's all true, when it comes down to it," the shrew agreed, fabulously drunk.

"That's the naked Truth," I insisted. "Come on, Onesta mia."

The evening's shadows deepened. A musical softness caused the air to vibrate like the taut strings of a zither.

Suddenly I shuddered. We heard resounding steps approaching. My vile companion was about to faint. I grabbed her arm and ordered her to follow me, as brutally as a cart driver who beats his animals. Even more passive than oxen, she obeyed.

It was a guard, whose massive build we could barely make out in the corridor filled with the half-light of dusk. I shivered feverishly when he called out to us, "Are you going for a breath of evening air along the canal?"

Onesta muttered, "My husband is a bit ill, Jacopo. We are both going to take a rest. Good night."

"Good night," repeated the man, who went on his way, humming.

We came to the large gate. The guard, in response to Onesta's choked request, opened the bars and let us go past him into the crepuscular blue. . . .

The southerly wind wafted aromatic memories and mysterious evil sensual delights. The lagoon was as tepid and perverse as uncovered sex organs. . . . I absent-mindedly caressed Onesta's dugs.

"Here is a gondola, my pensive beauty. Deign to follow me to the palace of my love dreams."

She embarked, drowned in a happy stupor. . . . I can navigate a small boat as easily as I can torture a woman, Gemma. I took the place of the slightly befuddled gondolier, and reassured the good chap by slipping him one of the pieces of gold that had been spared the jailers' greed.

We let ourselves be carried along the length of the mesmerizing canal. Oh, the cruelty of the waters and of the night!

A dwelling with wide-open doors dragged its red and yellow lights across the waves. The music of mandolins and scratchy guitars floated up to us from a tavern that was the haunt of sailors and gondolieri.

"Come, my immortal Lady. . . . There is some Asti spumante in the private rooms. . . ."

We entered. The stench of reeking garlic and bad wine suffocated me as soon as I crossed the threshold.

I drew the curtains in preparation for our imminent voluptuous pleasures. Onesta was already dozing off into a drunken stupor.

I thought about when she would wake up. When the alcohol was no longer fermenting in her empty brain, what terrors would dilate her half-witted pupils? She would denounce me. . . . And if, trusting to her torpor, I abandoned her right away, I feared the rekindling of some spark of intelligence.

And besides, why not admit it? I was filled with the cruelty of the waters and of the night. An inevitable rutting instinct made me just like a wildcat gone mad. I threw myself on the disgusting lush, and I used her with a frenzy that even your most sophisticated kisses, Gemma, have never whipped up in me. The violent pleasure made me sob feebly, like a plaintive child. And I bit those abject lips until they bruised.

But an even stronger lust assailed me. I took advantage of the stupor into which my companion was sinking, collapsing under the intensity of the climax, and seized her firmly by the throat, choking her in delight. . . . Certain short, fat necks are asking to be choked. . . .

Onesta's death throes were brief, too brief, even. Loaded down with wine, and weakened by her sexual convulsions, she quickly succumbed in my powerful hands. . . . I know how to strangle as skillfully as I know how to caress.

The grotesque hideousness of the corpse was so ridiculous that I began to laugh. The cooling of my carnal desires made me very gentle. The male in me was satisfied. A victim had been sacrificed to the cruelty of the waters and of the night. I left, my soul serene.

"Why are you leaving your companion here?" asked a barmaid, whom a sailor was fondling.

"She is too drunk to stand up. She is sleeping the sleep of the dead in their coffins."

And I smiled innocently at this joke, whose delicate flavor I alone could savor.

. . . The waters and the night approved of me and enveloped me with an indulgent gentleness. I spat at the reflection of the stars and sang my most beautiful songs to the sea.

A light, diaphanous hour passed. The reflections of the stars were extinguished in the depths of the lagoon. Then Dawn stridently burst forth, triumphant as a clarion call.

I rounded the Dogana Cape and followed the Giudecca Canal. The gondola's rocking motion gave a certain rhythm to my peaceful dreams. The green water had the treacherous languor of your sleepy eyes, Madonna. . . .

The gondola came to a stop in front of your door. Although the day had dawned, your house dozed in the shadows of sleep. The scent of indolence and delayed dreams reached me. I made my way toward your room.

You were sleeping. Your marble appearance made me freeze in my tracks. I trembled at the sight of your motionless eyelids. Your forehead, marbled by shadows, resembled the blueish foreheads of the Dead.

I stepped forward, my hands pressed together. I shivered, all my limbs frozen to the marrow. Slowly, slowly, you opened your eyes, Gemma mia. And in the depths of your wild eyes I saw such a monstrous terror that *I understood*. . . . I knew what invisible eyes had long ago hidden in the shadows in order to ambush me as I worked among my crucibles and my parchments. I knew which hand had scrawled those treacherous lines denouncing me to the Inquisition. . . . I knew who had betrayed me, out of curiosity about evil. . . .

. . . And it is from that day that you have loved me, Gemma mia. You love me with all your dread. Terror alone causes the trembling awakening of your weary body and soul. And because you fear me, you love me. You are not unaware that I will shatter you one day, when the mood takes me. You are not unaware that I will destroy you the moment you cease to please me. Silent with passive horror, you scrutinize my gestures and every step closely. . . . You await the End. But that moment has not yet come, for your body tempts me like the scented juice of watermelon and the flesh of ripe figs. Madonna Gemma, your hour has not yet sounded. . . .

I want your lips. . . . Kisses, kisses, kisses.

Forest Betrayal

Told by Blue Dirk

I'm not a wicked man, even though they call me the Forest Devil. They call me Blue Dirk, too, because I have tattoos all over my body. Joan was also blue with tattoos. Joan was my wife. We were never married according to the Anglican Church, because there was no clergyman where we first met, but she was my wife all the same.

She had the most beautiful tattoos that a woman could ever desire. No American Indian woman was ever more cleverly decorated with tomahawks and turtles. On her right leg, I had drawn her a devil with buffalo horns and a cow's tail. On her right wrist, a serpent like a bracelet. And above her left breast, two hearts pierced by a single arrow, with our initials intertwined.

I really don't understand why they called me the Forest Devil. It's true that I'm a bit mean when I've had too much to drink. I killed a couple of men unwittingly when I was drunk, and I've beaten up two or three women who resisted me when I wanted to violate them, the liquor having made me amorous. But I would never have done anything like that if I hadn't been drunk. It's also true that I forced myself on a little girl, but that only happened because I'd been wandering alone in the wastelands for a whole month without seeing a single woman, no matter how old or ugly. Honestly, I would never have behaved like that if I hadn't been so terribly deprived. As a sensual experience, it was pretty minimal. And besides, the child screamed so loudly. I left after I gave her a whack on the head. I don't like that screaming. Children should never be noisy. I did burn the feet of an old farmer's wife when she wouldn't tell me where she'd stashed the money. But since she ended up telling me where she'd hidden the nest egg, I didn't do her any more harm after that. Underneath it all, I'm really a model character. That smell of charring flesh was too hard to take anyway. In short, all of this is of no importance whatsoever, and I don't know why they call me the Forest Devil.

When it comes down to it, what is murder, anyway? It just advances the inevitable end by a few years. Is twenty minutes of torture really so terrible? Isn't it a thousand times less awful than long years of suffering? . . . Cancer, for example. . . . For myself, I would rather be assassinated than die of cancer. . . .

If I had ever dispatched to the other world someone who would have been immortal if not for me, then I certainly would have a load on my conscience.

As for the case of the little girl, all I did was anticipate the normal violence that, most likely, some other man would have done to her body. I've never possessed a pubescent virgin, but they tell me that the first time is always very unpleasant for the woman. So? Sooner or later, this little girl would have experienced a man's brutality one way or another.

It's true that a very large number of women die virgins. Even so, I've heard it said that this isn't a normal fate for a woman. It seems almost immoral, even. The people who have told me that are the kind who are called "healthy-minded." To have a healthy mind means you think the same way everyone else does.

Perhaps I was wrong to roast the feet of the old farmer's wife. But why did she have to be such a miser? If I was able to cure her of her stinginess, then I rendered her a great service. Perhaps I helped her enter the Kingdom of Heaven.

Underneath it all, I'm a model character. I'm going to prove it to you. When the inhabitants of a little Hindu village that was being ravaged by a pair of tigers came to me for help, I immediately went to their aid. It's true they offered me a handsome reward for ridding them of those two damned beasts. I assure you, though, that my love for my fellow man was the determining factor in my great undertaking.

Joan was with me . . . an admirable hunting companion. . . . That's exactly why I kept her around for so long.

One of the rare villagers who had escaped the claws of the tiger and tigress showed us their favorite haunt. We tethered a white calf to a nearby tree, and the following day Joan and I began our adventure.

We took with us the kullal,[1] who did double duty as both guide and water carrier, and bright-eyed Mangkali, my head shikari,[2] and Sala and Nursoo, two beaters who were a few years younger.

We had trekked several miles when we heard the tiger's magnificent roar. Joan shuddered almost voluptuously. Her eyes dilated with pride and enthusiasm. We were to confront an adversary worthy of us.

"Wuh hai!" wailed the kullal, who was trembling from head to foot and who had turned as green as old bronze, "that is the sahib of my village . . . the king of the land."

His abject terror was growing by the minute. Sensing that he was about to do something mad, Joan, with her usual calm, told him, "If you try to run away, the tiger will certainly have your skin, my friend. I advise you to stay behind us: it's your only chance of safety."

1. Wine merchant [*marchand de vin*; note in original text].
2. Beater [*rabatteur*; note in original text].

Mangkali and Joan led the way. Joan had the eyes of a lynx. We reached some rocks from which we could watch the sacrificial calf.

"Look," whispered Joan.

I looked. In the dusk, all I could see was a still, white mass.

"The calf is dead," Mangkali observed very quietly.

Joan merely waved her forefinger rhythmically in the air.

"Doom hilta hai,"[3] the youngest shikari, Nursoo, agreed. He had understood my wife's pantomime.

"Can you see the tiger?" I asked Joan.

She signaled that she could. Straining my eyes, I made out the shape of the animal at last.

Ah! What a superb beast!

Joan moved rapidly forward. I followed. The tiger was so busy devouring the unfortunate white calf alive that he did not hear us coming at all. We took cover behind a tree, twenty yards from the tiger.

The neck of the calf was disappearing down the maw of the beautiful monster, whose paws clutched cruelly at its victim.

---

3. "Its tail is still moving" ["Il remue encore la queue"; note in original text].

"Don't aim yet," Joan advised. "We mustn't wound him without killing him."

Making a supreme effort, the calf put up a struggle. The movement that its adversary made to regain his hold revealed the pale target of the tiger's belly and chest. I aimed at his heart and, a bit anxiously, I fired.

In one magnificent leap, he rolled, his jaws open, his breath coming in gasps. Joan approached the animal and with a blow of the rifle butt succeeded in breaking his spine. The kullal's teeth were chattering. Joan, who was irritated beyond all measure by his quaking cowardice, grabbed him impatiently by the arm.

"Come close and take a look," she said, pointing to the dead tiger. "He's a beautiful beast."

But the petrified kullal only moaned in terror. Joan pursed her lips in an expression of total disdain.

"Old man," she said to me, resting her rough killer's hand on my shoulder, "our work isn't finished. The tigress will certainly come back to join the tiger."

"You're right, Joan."

She did not take the weight of her hand off my shoulder. For the first time in my life, I saw her hesitate, sobered by the task ahead.

"It won't be easy," she said very slowly. "Maybe I'm being stupid, but I have an idea she's going to give us trouble. Female tigers are much more fearsome than male tigers, Dirk. They are more ferocious, and more treacherous."

"Are you trying to teach me my business? Surely you're not afraid. That would be a first. Still, if you don't want to go on with this. . . ."

"You know perfectly well, you idiot, that I'm not afraid of death. Since everyone has to go sometime, it's better to go in the open air, while one is young and strong, than to perish little by little in some suffocating, stinking sickroom. As for drugs—ugh! But I still think the tigress will give us trouble."

She gazed at the calm and beautiful forest. The branches of the trees looked like motionless pythons. The ropes of vine were coiled like green snakes. A breath of danger and betrayal rose from the earth and fell from the leaves. The stars were all out, like flaming flowers.

"How beautiful it all is!"

For the first time, Joan expressed a similar feeling. Usually, she was as resistant to wonder as she was to surprise and fear. Emotions offended her. She considered them signs of weakness.

"It's beautiful, very beautiful. And it makes me think about something I've never troubled about before. Dirk, is there anything beyond death?"

I groaned, not pleased. I really don't like talking about things I don't know anything about.

"Do you believe the clergyman was right when he said that there is another Self, and this Other Person doesn't die when the first one does?"

"You're annoying me, Joan."

"Too bad. I have to talk to someone this evening. I realize you won't understand me."

She stopped, with a faraway look.

"It's not that I'm afraid. Oh, no! But I do wonder why I don't know such a simple thing. And I also wonder why no one in the whole world, neither the soberest clergyman nor the best doctor, has ever found out such a simple thing. And it is, in the end, the only thing of any importance. How do you think that is, Dirk?"

"How should I know?"

"Naturally, you wouldn't know. You're not intelligent, but even if you were, it wouldn't make any difference. Dirk, we've hunted together for fifteen years. We've slept side by side. We've ended up looking like each other, just as we resemble each other in our souls. No matter how well you lie to me, you'll never succeed in taking me in. I understand you. You're not a bad man, and I'm not a bad woman. Oh, to be sure, we both have a few things on our conscience. Especially you. As for me, I have one thing to my credit: I've been a loyal and devoted hunting companion. Women are good, in general. But I'm not good, Dirk, because I'm too much like a man."

"You're talking as though you're going to die, Joan. You're annoying and stupid."

"It's odd to see how alone someone is when they're going to die. . . . They must be very cold. . . . I've never bothered about any of this before this evening. They must feel so very alone when they go Beyond! Do you think you'll meet anyone along the way, other souls who departed at the same time as you did?"

"Shut up, now."

"And then, too, they must feel so naked. No flesh, no bones. A mass without form or shape. They must float, like a cloud. That must be really unpleasant. And they wouldn't have a name anymore. They'd no longer be Joan, killer of tigers and wife of the Forest Devil. They aren't even a someone. They're a something. They wander around like that, in the void. They want to be someone, to become someone again, to have a name, to have a body to wear again. They are very alone and very naked and very cold."

"Will you shut up, once and for all?"

"Yes, I'll shut up, because I've said all I have to say."

We returned to the campsite. Joan, who had gone to fetch some water to boil in the kettle, didn't return. Some time passed.

"I would have heard her cry out if she'd been attacked by the tigress," I thought. "Oh, that bitch. Is she cheating on me with a Hindu?"

Then I thought that this was hardly likely. Joan wasn't a sensual woman and she despised the natives.

We went to look for her, going back along the road that led to the river. All at once, the shikari, Nursoo, shouted three times, "The tigress! The tigress! The tigress!" . . . And I heard the horrible caterwauling of the beast and the crunching of bone between her jaws.

There was nothing to be done. We had arrived too late. I understood what had happened. Lying in wait, the tigress had leapt on Joan and, burying her claws in her breast, she must have bitten her on the lips, preventing her from crying out for help. . . . Female tigers are as cunning as they are cruel, you know. . . .

So my poor Joan was devoured. I missed her for a long time, since she was such an excellent hunting companion. I'm neither soft nor a fool, but I will hear til the end of my life that fierce yet satisfied caterwauling, and the grinding of bone between her frightful jaws.

A Paradoxical Chastity

It was sheer chance that brought me to Genoa. I had been a guest in the city for three days, and though the journey there had been difficult and slow, it had in no way sapped my strength and courage, if you get my meaning. "Man is nothing but a dog in heat," said a wise man. . . . The lonely nights were starting to make me quite irritable. I resolved to find a mistress for an hour.

One of my friends, to whom I confided my needs, offered to take me to the house of the procuress Myriam, who was famous for her knack of arranging love affairs. Machiavelli himself would have been struck dumb in admiration. She had the most beautiful selection of women, and she understood her art royally.

Her palazzo had a fairy-tale reputation, and as I followed my friend to the house of the procuress, one quick look told me that my friend hadn't overpraised its splendors. We climbed a staircase made of purest marble, white as a glacier. The sculpting on the bronze banister represented trembling Hamadryads leaning over rivers and fountains to listen to the murmur of the

Naiads.[1] Austere statues lit up the half-shadows with their polished reflections.

Two Moorish servants preceded me into a vast room with deep-red velvet hangings. I observed more sculptures and a majestic fireplace. Immobile Vestal Virgins kept a watchful eye on the hearth. The light struck a painting in which two huntresses were carrying an offering killed with their triumphant bows to an image of Artemis.

The soft shades of the carpet evoked the entire world of lost Persia. The vases of pottery, of porcelain, and of wrought metal were miracles of workmanship. They were worthy of the flowers in them: a flamboyant summer of roses was wasting away in its own perfume. The immense picture window looked out on the sea, which shimmered beneath our bedazzled eyes, a glittering cascade of melted silver sprinkled with crystal.

A woman entered. Never had I seen a more generous beauty. She was bursting with the exotic magnificence of beautiful Jewish women. Pale with ecstasy, I contemplated the red and blue highlights of her black hair. Her eyes were the color of black grapes. The red velvet of the curtains and tapestries surrounded her

1. In Greek mythology, hamadryads are female spirits who inhabit trees, while naiads are female spirits who inhabit water.

with lively flames and intensified the muted fire of her balmy, fragrant flesh. Her mouth was as freshly red as a watermelon.

This woman was a living splendor. . . . She resembled the garden of a queen, a priceless jewel, a fabric ingeniously woven by patient hands. There was something serious and distant in her that inspired, or rather commanded, involuntary respect.

My friend bowed deferentially. "Myriam, allow me to present one of my friends," he said.

I stood there astounded. This creature, more beautiful than the most beautiful courtesan, was the procuress!

. . . She smiled. Jezebel must have smiled in this same shameless and royal fashion as she stood dusted with gold and gems.

"Signor, you will be dazzled," she promised as she disappeared behind the red cloud of the curtains.

My companion looked at me with curiosity.

"That's the one I want!" I cried, wild with wonder and amazement.

He shrugged his shoulders.

"Beware of turning your lusting eyes on her," he advised. "She is as inaccessible as a cold and snowy mountaintop."

"I don't recognize this joking tone of yours, my friend."

"But it's no joke. Myriam is chaste. The word is that she is a virgin. She trafficks in the virtue of others, but she keeps her own intact all the while. She understands the value of what others sell or give away too lightly. Besides, her occupation must have given her a horror or disgust of men. Let me repeat: put any thought of her out of your mind."

Shrugging off this idiotic remark, I uttered an impatient exclamation. . . . Just at that moment, the doors opened wide, and a bevy of young women, as rosy as the Graces, entered, buzzing and swarming. The air filled with fragrance. But I had eyes only for Myriam, the black sun among the stars. Never had I understood quite so deeply and intensely, never had I truly felt and loved the proud prestige of brunettes.

"Allow me to present Myrtô the Sicilian," Myriam said. "Her flesh has the scent of ripe apples. And this is Violante, a flower of Spain. She is as lovely as her name. And this is Lollia, who plays the guitar as skillfully as a Venetian. And this is Néis, who dances like a Faun. Here is Néméa, as blond as gold in the sun."

"I love blonds," stated my friend. "And that one is as light as you could ever hope for. What foamy whiteness!"

He followed Néméa, who led him away.

Noticing my lack of enthusiasm for her female following, Myriam murmured in my ear: "If you long for someone highly placed, I will introduce you to a marchioness who has a heroic lineage. But before she will remove her mask, she demands that you swear to the Holy Virgin that you will never say a word about it. She is beautiful but poor."

I refused with a gesture.

"I can guess what you're thinking. You are in love, but the woman resists. Whisper to me, my handsome gentleman, the name of this indifferent woman. No one knows as well as I do how to express persuasive and suggestive language. Even if she is as cold as a statue, I will lead her to you in a few days. And if she persists in her stony, icy frigidity, I will find you a young woman just like her, who resembles her feature for feature, but one who will be softer and more amenable to your desires."

I stared at her. She had put her hand on my arm, but her cool touch burned me. Myriam's voice became even more insinuating.

"I would like to speak with you alone," I brusquely interrupted.

She smiled with her whole brown face. "Leave us, my doves."

The gracious forms vanished.

From my finger I removed a very rare ruby, which was as beautiful as the blood of a wounded woman, and I threw it, along with my heavy purse, on the onyx table.

"Take them, Myriam, and take this sapphire, too, as blue as the Mediterranean. In exchange, give me your most expert kisses."

She smiled again, but with a sharper smile. "You are mistaken, sir," she replied very calmly. "I am the merchant, not the merchandise."

I met her haughty look.

"You are a first-rate coquette," I laughed nervously. "But you please me. I'll pour all the gold you want into your hands."

"I sell others, not myself."

Mad with desire, I pulled her against me. "Love me, for I love you."

And I planted my feverish kiss on her cold lips.

She took a step back, and, tearing herself from my embrace, she slapped me in the face so violently that I staggered.

"Leave," she ordered.

But my male vanity protested, and I resolved to force this woman to submit to my wishes. I approached her, my senses so inflamed that I was ready to violate. My hand reached for her untamed breasts that heaved impetuously from her angry breathing.

Swifter than a swallow's flight, she seized a stiletto dagger, a filigreed and jeweled marvel that hung decoratively from her belt, and she plunged it into my breast. . . . I fell. . . . An acute pain pierced my heart. . . . I sank into the depths of a red night. . . .

It was with great difficulty that the most skillful doctors were able to pull me out of Death's tenacious grip. I recovered thanks to the marvel of my vigorous youthfulness.

Never again did I cross the threshold of the procuress, that strange woman, perverse and pure, shameless and inaccessible. . . .

The Splendid Prostitute

The story of an Envious Person[1]

. . . And Glory appeared unto me. I caught a glimpse of her eyes, the color of copper, and of her hair, the color of blood. This apparition surprised me a little, for I had scarce hoped to profit from her fickle favors. But Glory is a woman—that is, cruel and perverse, and she loves to flash her star-spangled skirt in front of those she scorns.

I braced myself, in order to contemplate her without love but with all my pride and contempt. Then I carefully addressed her in familiar tones: "Don't think for one minute that my house is a hut where people can drag in vials of cheap perfume and pots of makeup. What are you doing in this empty bedroom that contains only memories? Why do you want to dazzle me, a has-been? . . . I see you for what you are. I turned away from

1. Although not named explicitly, the "envieux" (note the masculine form of the adjective) who narrates this encounter with Glory would seem to reflect the attitudes of Vivien herself. The narrator reproaches Glory for remembering ultimately insignificant military heroes while failing to protect the memory of notable female poets of ancient Greece, a sentiment that Vivien surely shared.

you because you made me sick to my stomach.[2] You are the drunken mistress of thieves and charlatans. You love the stench of slaughterhouses and you take pleasure in inhaling the precious fumes of blood. You are as blind as those who make a profession of judging their neighbors. You are as stupid as a warrior and as venal as a tinseled whore. You prefer to abandon yourself to those who violate you, and if by chance you elevate a poor man or a proud woman, it is only out of the caprice of an intoxicated courtesan. In truth, the whole public has free access to your sexual favors, and I, for one, would not care to welcome such an ugly whore into my bed."

"You're bluffing like a child," she answered. "I haven't the slightest intention of abandoning myself to you. . . . Besides, you know you would slit your wrists for my mercenary kiss. It's your foolish vanity that makes you think you wouldn't. But you are controlled by vanity, the same as everyone else."

"On the other hand," I interrupted, "what wretched joy makes someone invent legends about herself in which the evil is matched only by the foolishness! Oh, the poi-

2. Until this point, the narrator has been speaking in the *passé simple* tense in French, which does not require subject agreements, meaning that the sex of the narrator is not indicated, but here the narrator uses the *passé composé* tense, which requires subject agreements, and an extra "e" ending reveals the speaker to be female.

soned words that creep into your veins and flow in your blood! . . . You are less of a Whistle-blower of secret faults than you are a Slanderer. You are the one who privately dishonors all those you raise up in public."

"Perhaps you are right. But there are good and sentimental people who hope, through their writings and their works, to attract kindred spirits to their lonely condition, either now or at some point in the future."

"They are only kindred spirits as long as they remain undiscovered," I objected. "I never met one single person in the whole world without later regretting having understood them too well and known them too long."

"You're lying again, because I have seen by your side a woman whose indulgent sweetness has made you weep with love."

"This time you're right. Anyone who has met a loyal woman along his path should no longer seek or desire anything more. But what do you care about my life and thought, you who are the battered servant of butchers and soapbox barkers? You who carve in marble the insignificant names of kings while scorning the names of good, if obscure, poets? You who place Hugo,[3] the

3. Victor Hugo is remembered today more for his novels, such as *Les Misérables* (1862), than for his plays and his poetry, whose style had fallen somewhat out of favor by Vivien's day. In his youth, however, he was known as a dramatist who had played a leading role in

prince of the bourgeoisie, higher than Rimbaud[4] and Charles Cros?[5] And most important of all, you who allowed the sacred chants of Myrtis[6] the Ionian, those of the heroic Telesilla,[7] and especially those of the melodious, virginal Eranna of Telos to perish?[8] Even your servants have an unacknowledged scorn for your caresses. They return to their manuscripts or their canvas with disgust, like the dog in Scripture returns to his

the Romantic movement through his controversial play *Hernani* (1830) and for his opposition to Napoleon III, expressed in poetry such as *Les châtiments* (1853; *The Punishments*). At his death in 1885, he was granted a state funeral in Paris, where he was mourned by millions.

4. The symbolist poet Arthur Rimbaud was a precocious talent who did his best work before the age of twenty. By the mid 1870s he had turned his back on poetry and left France, and few people had heard of him. His fame came later, when his work was published in the *Mercure de France*. He remains one of the foremost French poets, and his work has influenced many subsequent musicians, writers, and artists, such as John Ashbery, Jim Morrison, and Patti Smith. An edition of Rimbaud's *Poésies complètes* (*Complete Poems*), with a preface by Paul Verlaine (Léon Vanier, 1895), is known to have figured among Vivien's books (Albert and Rollet 189).

5. Charles Cros, less well known today than Hugo or Rimbaud, nevertheless enjoyed a reputation as a talented poet during his lifetime.

6. Myrtis was a Greek poet of the sixth century BCE. She was reputed to be the teacher of the poet Corinna, the second most important woman poet of ancient Greece after Sappho. Vivien translated some of her poetry in *Les kitharèdes* (*The Kitharedes*).

7. Telesilla was another ancient Greek woman poet translated by Vivien.

8. Little is known about the ancient Greek poet Erinna, but she is thought to have been born at Telos. She is also featured in *The Kitharedes*.

own vomit. Like opium addicts and drunkards, they are damned to an incurable vice. Really, go away. . . . Night is falling, as beautiful as impending Death. And the hope of a short and painless passing consoles those who sit in the shadows."

The Ladysaurus

Told by Mike Watts

The sun is terrible. The sun is worse than plague and wild animals and gigantic black snakes. It's worse than fever. It's a thousand times worse than death.

The sun has scorched the back of my neck and my temples and my skull; it has dried and bleached my hair like grass during sweltering heat. Anyone else but me would have gone mad on those long treks through the desert. At times it felt like molten lead was running down my forehead and along my arms and legs. Oh! Oh! Anyone else but me would have gone mad, but I have a good strong head and body. I have seen some people howling and waving their arms like demons after those long days of marching through the desert. The sun pounding on their imbecile brains gave them some strange ideas. But not me—I have always been calm and reasonable.

. . . The sun was terrible.

Toward the end of one afternoon when the long, sharp rays of the sun were still raining down like javelins, I came across a very strange woman. I'm no coward, but this woman scared me because of her horrifying resemblance to a crocodile.

Don't think for a moment that I'm mad. I've got all my wits; I even have quite a solid reputation for good sense. I swear to you that this woman resembled a crocodile.

She had a rough, scaly skin. Her tiny eyes terrified me. Her enormous mouth terrified me even more, with its sharp, equally enormous teeth. I swear, this woman looked exactly like a crocodile.

She was staring into the water when I got up the courage to approach her.

"What are you looking at there?" I asked her, since I was both curious and secretly appalled at the same time.

She fastened her tiny, terrible reptilian eyes on mine. Instinctively, I recoiled.

"I'm looking at the crocodiles," she answered. "I'm sort of related to them. I know all their habits. I call them by name. And they recognize me when I walk by on the riverbank."

She spoke in such a simple, natural tone of voice that I shuddered with an icy terror. I knew that *she was telling the truth*. I didn't dare to stare at her rough, scaly skin.

"The king and queen of the crocodiles are my personal friends," she continued. "The king lives at Dendera.[1] The queen, who is just as powerful and even more cruel, preferred to go forty leagues higher up the river so that she could reign by herself. She wants undivided power. He loves his independence too; which means that they live separately, while remaining very good friends. They meet only occasionally, in order to make love."

I saw in her eyes a gleam of ferocious lust that made my teeth start to chatter. I'm using this cliché deliberately, because at that moment I really understood it in all its strength and horror. The awful sun pressed down and flattened me with its giant weight. Its liquid fire scorched me. Nevertheless, my teeth chattered against each other as though it was winter, when the freezing cold numbs your blood.

"I believe you," I chattered.

She came up to me with an awkward, sluggishly slithering motion. . . . The simperings of this monster were more terrifying than her deformity.

"No, you don't believe me. What's your name?"

"Mike Watts."

---

1. Dendera: a small town situated on the west bank of the Nile, in Egypt.

"All right, Mike, I swear to you that I can ride a crocodile just like riding a horse. Do you believe me?"

I was sweating even more profusely than before, only now it was a cold sweat that froze my limbs.

"Yes, I believe you."

And I did in fact believe her. I'm not crazy. I've never been crazy, even in the desert, even when I was suffering from thirst. But I did believe her, and you would have believed her too, just as I did.

She smirked in a horrible way—that is, she opened her mouth. . . . She opened her great, big, disgusting caiman muzzle and silently showed me all her teeth. A shiver ran through my entire body, and there it all was. . . . Oh, God who invented hell!

"No, you don't believe me," the Ladysaurus repeated. "But I'm going to prove what I'm saying."

She inspected the yellowish river, flowing with sand and silt.

"There's one," she said very quietly. "Step back."

I didn't wait for her to repeat the command. I took off. But I stopped a short distance away from the river, suddenly bound by something even more compelling than terror itself.

. . . *At the very moment that the crocodile was about to snap shut its jaws, I saw her hoist herself on its back, and, for the time it takes to have a nightmare, I saw her riding astride an alligator. . . .*

I'm not raving. I'm in my right mind. I'm not lying, either. Lying is all very well for civilized men. The rest of us never tell lies. We can't deal with the complications.

The crocodile lady came back toward me, leaving the crocodile moving sluggishly in the brackish water. She came back, her eyes gleaming with triumph—and with something else again. . . .

She was expecting some expression of surprise and approval. . . . But I was staggering like a drunk, and I could only mouth incoherent syllables—buh, buh, buh—and I was drooling like an idiot.

She looked at me with eyes that held all the ferocious lust of a monster in rut.

"Come here," she ordered.

I tried to follow her. I couldn't do it. I could only make the choked gestures of a madman confined in a straitjacket.

A few steps away from where we stood there was a tangle of very tall grass and trees whose branches looked like giant snakes. She kept glancing over at this cover. . . . It was obvious what she wanted from me. . . .

. . . It's very hard for me to explain to you what I was going through at that moment. All kinds of ideas were racing through my mind, like a pack of mad dogs. I knew I had to kill the monster, but how . . . how?

. . . Bullets and steel would bounce off her hide without doing her any harm. All right, didn't she have any weak spots anywhere else? No. . . . Of course . . . her eyes . . . *her eyes*!

A fevered and delirious joy seized hold of me, the kind of joy felt only by those who have been shipwrecked and then step onto dry land once again, or by the sick who finally see the dawn dispel their nighttime hallucinations. I danced; I managed to swallow my saliva; I even babbled out my impressive array of stupid love talk.

I emptied my wineskin at one gulp. The thought of my impending deliverance ran through my veins, along with the benevolent warmth of the brandy. . . . Now I had the strength to perform the deadly business. . . . And, while the Ladysaurus awaited her carnal satisfaction with her pupils rolled back in her drunken eyes, I grabbed my knife and, attacking the monster who was sprawling on the grass, I poked out her eyes. . . .

I poked out her eyes, I tell you. Oh, one thing I am is courageous, that's for sure! You can quibble about me, but you can never make me out to be a coward. Lots of men in my situation would have lost their heads. But me, I didn't hesitate for a second. . . .

And, as I was leaving there, I went back to look at the yellowish river, heavy with sand and silt, one last time.

The Veil of Vashti

As innocent as Christ, who died for men, she devoted herself for women.

—Gustave Flaubert,
The Temptation of St. Anthony

In the house of King Ahasuerus, Queen Vashti prepared a feast for the women.[1]

The court of the palace glittered like the setting sun. The flagstones, embedded with mother-of-pearl and hematites, were covered with the blood of rose petals. The columns of marble were draped with garlands of datura.[2] Above the golden beds shimmered green, blue,

1. The story of Vashti, queen of Persia and the first wife of the Persian king Ahasuerus, is told in the biblical Book of Esther (1:9–22). The usual interpretation of Vashti's behavior is that she was sinfully proud of her beauty and therefore rightly punished and replaced by Queen Esther, but there was a growing sense in nineteenth-century feminist circles that wives might not always owe their tyrannical husbands blind obedience and that Vashti acted out of exemplary modesty. In Charlotte Brontë's novel *Villette* (1853), an independent-minded character based on the French actress Rachel (Elisabeth Félix) is named Vashti, for example.

2. The datura, or moonflower, is a poisonous plant with trumpet-shaped flowers. The flowers and seeds can cause hallucinations, and in some folklore traditions, a person who falls asleep under a datura will wake up insane.

and white tapestries that hung from ropes of sea silk[3] attached to silver rings.

The feast lasted seven days. The slaves poured drinks into malachite vessels, each one differently carved, and there was an abundance of royal wine.

On the seventh day, Vashti, who was surrounded by the princesses of Persia and of Media, and by the wives of the noblemen and of the provincial leaders, listened to the women Musicians. They sang of the power and the wisdom of the queens of India, who had sea-green serpents for lovers.

Vashti's face was as beautiful as the night. Her proud brows arched triumphantly. Her eyelids were lowered, solemn as the violet eyelids of Sleep. And her black eyes, in which all of Ethiopia shone, were vast, unknown countries.

The Musicians stopped playing. An old Jewish slave woman recounted the legend of Eblis and of a certain Lilith, who was created before Eve and who was the First Woman.

". . . And Lilith, scorning the love of man, preferred the embrace of the Serpent. This is why Lilith was punished

3. Sea silk is a form of rare and expensive fabric made from the byssus, or filaments, of certain species of mussels.

for centuries. Several have seen her, by the melancholy light of the moon, crying over dead serpents. She is like the supernatural dreams of hermits. She torments honest sleep with dreams. She is Fever, she is Desire, she is Perversity. In truth, Lilith has been punished for centuries because nothing will ever appease her hunger for the Absolute."

"I would like to have been Lilith," Queen Vashti mused out loud.

"Eblis, like his mortal companion, is cursed, O Sovereign. Eblis is the fallen star that sinks in the darkness because he dreamed of being the equal of God."

"I would like to have been Eblis," Queen Vashti mused out loud.

"Eblis is the foremost among the vanquished, O Sovereign . . . because Eblis desired the Impossible."

"I love the vanquished," murmured Vashti. "I love all those who attempt the Impossible."

The old Jewish woman, who had the wisdom of the ages, seemed to draw into herself. Vashti tore a pink lotus into shreds.

. . . A roar of laughter shook the marble columns and made the mother-of-pearl and the porphyry of the flagstones tremble. It was the courtiers, intoxicated thanks to the king's munificence. The king, whose heart was gladdened by the wine, encouraged them.

Vashti lowered her eyelids in order to conceal the scorn that glimmered in the depths of her Ethiopian eyes. Her skin exuded spices and the oil of myrrh and the perfumes used among the women.

The green, white, and blue hangings parted to allow someone to enter. . . . Vashti covered her face with a gray veil that was encrusted with beryls. It was the color of twilight by the sea.

The seven eunuchs who served King Ahasuerus entered with silent steps. The princesses of Persia and of Media stopped whispering and murmuring. . . . The eunuchs kneeled at the feet of Queen Vashti and let her know the order of King Ahasuerus. Vashti gazed at them through her gray veil with eyes like the bored eyes of lions.

In the silence that followed the words of the messengers, they heard a rose drop its petals.

Vashti got up from her golden bed. Tall and proud, she spoke: "O princesses of Persia and of Media, King Ahasuerus has ordered Mehuman, Biztha, Harbona, Bigtha, Abagtha, Zethar, and Carcas—the seven eunuchs who serve King Ahasuerus—to bring Queen Vashti into his royal presence wearing her royal crown, in order to show her beauty to the common people and to the nobility. . . ."

There was a tense silence. In truth, the order of King Ahasuerus was something that had no precedent in the history of the Persians nor of the Medians, nor in the history of India, nor in the history of the Ethiopians. Because the impure glance of men should never profane the mystery of the female face.

Vashti resumed talking very slowly.

"Here is the answer of Queen Vashti to King Ahasuerus: *When Queen Vashti received the order of King Ahasuerus from the eunuchs, Queen Vashti refused to go.*"

The eunuchs withdrew. Every face fell. A Persian princess dropped the cup from which she had been drinking, and the king's wine spread over the porphyry and the mother-of-pearl flagstones. . . . The king's wine spread, red as a stream of blood. The old Jewish woman tore her robe and beat her chest: "Woe upon you and upon us, O Queen!"

Stiff as a marble statue with eyes of black stones, Vashti spoke thus to the princesses of Persia and of Media: "I will never unveil my sacred face in front of a crowd of drunken courtiers. The impure stares of men must never profane the mystery of my face. The order of King Ahasuerus is an outrage to my pride as a woman and as a queen."

The old Jewish woman, seizing a censer in which incense was burning, covered her white head with ashes and lamented: "Rebellion is a deadly thing, O Queen! Think about the rebellion of Eblis. . . . Think about the rebellion of Lilith. . . . Think about the eternal punishment of Lilith and Eblis!"

"What does it matter!" said Queen Vashti then. And she spoke these solemn words: "It was not just King Ahasuerus that I was thinking about when I acted. . . . For my action will reach all women, and they will say: *King Ahasuerus had ordered Queen Vashti to be brought into his presence, and she did not go.* And from this day on, the princesses of Persia and of Media will know that they are no longer the servants of their husbands, and that the man is no longer the master of his house, but that the woman is free and a mistress who is equal to the master in his house."

The princesses of Persia and of Media rose and looked at one another with new eyes in which the pride of being set free shone.

The old Jewish woman was still lamenting. . . .

The green, white, and blue hangings parted for a second time. And the seven eunuchs of King Ahasuerus reappeared.

The seven eunuchs, Mehuman, Biztha, Harbona, Bigtha, Abagtha, Zethar, and Carcas, spoke to Queen Vashti as follows: "O Queen, when the king heard the answer of Queen Vashti to King Ahasuerus, the king was very irritated; in fact, he began burning with rage. Then the king appealed to the wise men who have the wisdom of the ages. He had by him Carschena, Schethar,

Admatha, Tarsis, Meres, Marsena, Memucan—seven princes of Persia and of Media, who are in the king's inner circle and who are the foremost men in his kingdom. *What law,* said he, *should I apply to Queen Vashti for not having obeyed King Ahasuerus's order as conveyed by his eunuchs?* Memucan addressed the king and the princes: *It is not only with respect to the king that the queen has behaved badly: it's also toward all the princes and all the common men who are in all the provinces of King Ahasuerus. This is because the action of the queen will come to be known by all the wives and will cause them to scorn their husbands. They will say: 'King Ahasuerus had ordered Queen Vashti to be brought into his presence, and she did not go.' And from this day on, the princesses of Persia and of Media, who will have been informed of the action of the queen, will spread it to all the chiefs of the king; much contempt and anger will come from that. If the king feels it right, let him proclaim, and let it be written down among the laws of the Persians and Medians—with no one allowed to transgress it—a royal decree according to which Vashti will never appear before King Ahasuerus, and the king will give the title of queen to another who is better than she. The edict of the king will be known throughout the kingdom—no matter how big it is—and all the women will honor their husbands, from the noblest right down to the humblest.*

"The king and the princes judged in favor of this opinion."

The princesses of Media and Persia wept in silence.

Vashti arose and with a haughty gesture removed the royal crown from her hair. She also removed the pearls from her neck, the pale sapphires from her fingers, the beryls from her arms and the emeralds from her waist. She took off her gown of purple linen and put on the torn tunic that belonged to the old Jewish woman. Then she crowned her head with pink lotuses and wrapped her entire body in her dusky veil.

"Where are you going, Mistress?" sobbed the old Jewish woman, prostrating herself before her.

"I am heading for the desert where human beings are as free as the lions."

"No man has ever returned from the desert, Mistress, and no woman has ever ventured there."

"Perhaps I shall perish there of hunger. Perhaps I shall perish there in the jaws of wild animals. Perhaps I shall die there of loneliness. But, since the rebellion of Lilith, I am the first free woman. My action will come to be known by all women, and all those who are slaves in their husband's or father's house will secretly envy me. Thinking about my glorious rebellion, they will say: 'Vashti scorned being queen in order to be free.'"

And Vashti set off for the desert where dead serpents come back to life under the moonlight.

The Nut-Brown Maid

In this story, Vivien appears to be conflating two sources. "The Nut-Brown Maid," or "The Nut-Brown Maiden," is a traditional ballad included by Thomas Percy in his anthology Reliques of Ancient English Poetry *(1765). A three-volume edition of this work (Swan Sonnenschein, 1889) is among the books from Renée Vivien's personal collection now in the Bibliothèque Historique de la Ville de Paris (Albert and Rollet 193). This (English) version dwells on the theme of women's fidelity. A man tests his would-be lover's constancy by telling her he has been outlawed and must take to the woods. The woman agrees to follow him. He warns her that the conditions will test her love and that, among other things, she will have to disguise herself as a man; endure harsh conditions; and face slander, punishment, and even death if caught. Nell in this story seems to take after this woman, suggesting that Percy's is the model Vivien had in mind. There is also a Scottish ballad called "My Nut-Brown Maiden," but the lyrics are merely about a man who misses his brown-eyed girlfriend, whom he hopes to see soon. Jerry describes Nell as having nut-brown eyes (and hair), but she is also tanned from spending so much time outdoors. This is in contrast to the valorization of fair, white skin as part of the ideal of female beauty at the time, since tanned skin was associated with outdoor work and therefore with manual, lower-class labor.*

Nell was indeed a perfect adventure companion. She was as brave and as vigorous as a boy and more intelligent.

I loved her very much and wanted to make her my mistress. But she wasn't having it.

Why? How would I know, as someone who has never had the time to study women? And besides, women get on my nerves. I don't understand a thing about their ways. I prefer wild animals. At least wild animals let themselves be taken, and once you've got them, they're done and that's that. Whereas with women, good God! . . . once you've caught them, you have to keep them. And the thing is, you can't keep them. You have to be especially careful when they tell you they love you. When they don't say anything, then it's possible that they like you. But it's still not for sure. When they tell you they hate you, chances are it isn't true. But it might also be the involuntary admission of the secret hatred that all women, consciously or unconsciously, feel toward men. Now I'm talking just like a book. And all this to keep rehashing the same point, which is that, all things considered, when it comes to women, everything is possible and nothing is certain.

Me, I'm not wily. As a result, I haven't gotten into it as often as the others who are. You'd best not be wily with women. They always notice it, but since they are cleverer than you, they pretend not to see it. And so, without you knowing a thing about it, they'll put on an amazing little act for you. And you're taken in by it. I really pity many men who boast about their female conquests. It means they've been cuckolded without even knowing it, poor fellows!

. . . Nell wasn't a real woman. Still, she wasn't ugly. She had a beautiful brow and beautiful eyelids. I like long, arched feet and long, thin hands. I hate little feet, ill suited to really long walks, and little hands that don't know how to handle either a revolver or a rifle. In general, women are quite a nuisance. But then Nell wasn't a real woman.

I don't know why she wasn't the least interested in becoming my mistress. Deep in the woods there are no moral scruples. It was just that she was resistant to love. There are many women who have an instinctive horror of males. It isn't that she had some profound hatred of me personally. On the contrary, she had professed a fraternal love for me. When I injured my hand, she dressed it better than a nun: she consoled me in a friendly way with all sorts of gentle words.

"My poor old friend," she kept saying, though I was only thirty years old back then. . . .

I will never forget her eyes, brown as hazelnuts, and her short hair the color of sand. I called her the Nut-Brown Maid, in memory of an old Scottish ballad. She too was a virgin, brown as a hazelnut.

As I was saying, she loved me very much as a friend, as a comrade, as a hunting partner. But when I tried to make her share the sneaking desire that had crept into my veins bit by bit, I ran up against her rigid will, which was like an iron wall. At those moments, she looked at me with such a wild horror in her eyes and with such a total, suddenly hostile, repulsion that I had to back off. The only things that pleased her were the outdoors, walks through the forest, wildflowers gathered from the path, and danger and adventure. She was made for danger and adventure just as much as I was. We loved one another like brothers. At the heart of our friendship, which was nevertheless real, lurked the putrid slime of suspicion, hatred even. She defied me, and I couldn't put aside my fierce resentment at being a rejected male. Men are pigs, you know, simply pigs; moreover, that's the only way they are superior to women, who are weak enough to make the mistake of being good. . . . I'll never forgive Nell for not having the slightest desire to be my mistress. . . . I'll never forgive her, even on my deathbed.

One incident in particular vexed me. One green evening we were in the middle of the forest when I tried to kiss her on the mouth. She punched me right between the eyes with such a tremendous whack that I was disfigured for over two weeks . . . two weeks during which my hunting buddies teased me mercilessly. But that wasn't all. She added insult to the physical injury she caused.

"I'd rather swallow a toad than let you kiss me," she said, pointing to the tiny brown creature that had suggested to her this hardly flattering comparison.

An idea, a cowardly one I confess, but ingenious all the same, crossed my mind. Despite being in pain, I abandoned myself to a frantic chase that resulted in the capture of the little toad.

"Swallow it immediately," I ordered, "or I'll kiss you by force."

She looked me right in the eye. Her solemn expression told me that she understood I wasn't joking in the least. An expression of unutterable scorn crept over her thin lips, the lips of an ascetic, a hermit. She took the horrid little creature and swallowed it, turning just a little bit paler.

This casual deed discouraged me. I no longer tried to kiss her. I held a deadly grudge against her.

One day she came up to me, her hazelnut eyes even clearer and more joyful than usual.

"I have a superb plan to put to you, dear old Jerry.[1] You know I'm infinitely fond of you, even if I did choose to swallow a toad rather than kiss you. I'm going to prove

1. The words "dear old Jerry" are in English in the original.

my friendship to you by taking you along with me this evening. At sunset, we'll set off together in a canoe. We'll take a torch to light our way. And we'll have a great hunt by this magnificent light—just the two of us. We'll kill lots of deer before tomorrow morning."

"I'm all for that," I agreed. And that very evening, we set off in a canoe that an old Indian lent to Nell.

What an unforgettably wonderful time! The torchlight turned the river to blood with scarlet reflections. You would have thought you saw a palace of flames in the water. The two banks were bursting with blood orange. The trees sprouted red foliage as if it were October. . . . It was as beautiful as the landscape of hell, except that instead of the damned, there was only me. And I don't think I've committed a big enough sin to have merited that splendid show.

"Over there!" whispered Nell urgently. With her outstretched finger she pointed to the right bank. I saw two large pupils reflecting the red light.

"A deer," I declared exultantly. I seized my rifle and, aiming between the two luminous eyes, I fired. We heard a rustling of leaves and of reeds, and then the water shook from a loud crash.

Nell let out a cry of joy when we discovered a superb buck, which I grabbed by its antlers and hoisted triumphantly into the canoe.

Nell took hold of the paddle again, and we continued down the river in silence.

It was a beautiful yellow night. The shadows seemed like very thick layers of amber. The moon flowed like melting gold lava. At the bottom of the river, the stars were shining like the spangles of a Harlequin's skirt.

Something sentimental foolishly whimpered within me. If the story of that toad hadn't still been running through my head, I would have loved Nell at that moment with such a tender passion. I don't know how to turn out fancy sentences, but I would have taken her hand in mine, and I would have become a better person. I would no longer be angry or hate anyone. I would have pardoned that Indian who stole my silver watch. I would have even pardoned *her* for the idiotic love she was making me suffer. I would have become credulous and trusting, like a little child. For her and because of her, I would have carried out selfless good deeds. I would have done favors for people. I would have stopped fighting, even with the Tuscaroarers.[2] To get closer to her, I would have become gentle like her. Yes, I would have stopped being brave in order to be good, and isn't that the greatest sacrifice that one can make for a woman?

2. The Tuscarora, a North American tribe.

. . . In the shadows, I half saw Nell's beautiful brow and lowered eyelids. Calling myself a fool, with good reason, I felt myself becoming as stupid as a poetry book.

The low voice of the Nut-Brown Maid interrupted my hopeless reverie.

"Look at those eyes staring at us through the bushes! Did you see those eyes, Dirk?[3] Those aren't the eyes of a deer. . . . They shine in a completely different way; what's more, they're smaller and further apart. . . . Did you see them, over there? How they shine through the bushes!"

"You're right, Nell."

"Now, see how they're moving! The eyes of a deer don't move like that. Deer don't move their heads in irregular circles like that. Their eyes dart rapidly from one thing to another, or stare intently. . . . Deer don't have such indecisive and flickering eyes at all, Jerry."

My rifle disturbed the river and the night with a short, sharp thunderclap.

---

3. Elsewhere, the narrator's name is Jerry, but here Nell calls him Dirk, the name of the character in "Forest Betrayal." This seems to be a lapse on the part of Vivien. Although she proofread her work carefully (see Goujon), she does not seem to have caught this inconsistency. In a series of letters from early 1904, she sent her corrections of the page proofs of *La dame à la louve* to her publisher (Albert and Rollet 202–03). In a letter of April 1904, she lists, page by page, the changes she wants made to pages 133–200 of the proofs, a range that includes the story "Brune comme une noisette," but she makes no mention of correcting the name Dirk.

Nell screamed at me, "Don't shoot, you idiot!"

But it was too late. The shot was fired.

We looked toward the bank. To my great surprise, the eyes were still staring at us through the bushes. But they shone with an angry red light.

Expecting some explanation of this mystery, I turned to Nell.

We heard what sounded like a furiously grunting pig. I felt myself blanch. Even the Nut-Brown Maid became slightly flustered.

We were dealing with a grizzly bear. . . .

"Your bullet definitely hit him," Nell murmured. "Let's just hope he doesn't attack us!"

The crackling of leaves . . . a sudden and heavy dive . . . Nell's fears were realized. The bear was swimming after us.

With all her strength and with all her courage, Nell propelled the canoe forward. We glided rapidly over the river, pursued by the roaring and snorting bear.

We were engulfed in the uncertainty of night.

"If he catches up to us," said Nell very calmly, "the canoe will capsize under his weight. We'll have to swim, like the bear, and one of us will never make it to the bank."

I had the very understandable hope that she would be the one. . . . We were unarmed. Our rifles had slid to the bottom of the boat, and the water had put them out of commission. . . . And, by a devilish stroke of bad luck, I couldn't locate my knife.

I turned toward the young woman whose paddle tirelessly plowed through the water. Suddenly, she sat bolt upright with a nervous jump.

"Listen, Jerry. . . ."

Our apprehensive eyes met. We heard the noise of falling water.

"That must be the waterfall that we heard higher up, at the bend of the river," I ventured.

"No . . . the noise is very near. Jerry, Jerry, the waterfall is no more than a hundred meters away. . . . Use the butt of your rifle as a paddle and help me stop the canoe."

We succeeded in slowing down the light craft, and we entertained hopes of steering it toward the bank when a heavy crash rocked the back of the boat. The flickering torch revealed to us the head and long, curved claws of the bear. The instability of the canoe, which was bobbing frantically and threatening to flip bottom up, didn't discourage the tenacious bear one jot, but gave us a moment's respite from the falls.

Nell looked at me with her indomitable eyes.

"Are you afraid, Jerry? Me, I'm not at all afraid. . . . Maybe the end will be quick. . . . I've always felt a lot of affection for you, my brother Jerry."

A burst of love, as violent as despair, propelled me toward her.

"Since we're both about to die, my dear, my beloved . . . since we'll be dead in ten minutes, in five minutes, in three minutes maybe . . . give me your lips. . . . Let me kiss you on the mouth . . . and I'll die happier than I've lived. I'll even be content to die."

She was pure and hostile like one of those little sea creatures that live tucked inside a shell with mother-of-pearl walls. . . . I saw the pained contraction of her entire brown face.

"I can't, Jerry. Even faced with the great shadows, I can't . . . and yet I love you very much, my brother Jerry. . . ."

This was even more bitter than the idea of death. . . . I was indeed incredibly stupid that evening, even more so than usual.

She rapidly regained her self-control.

"All hope is not lost, Jerry. We mustn't die without having fought Death."

With a disheartened gesture, I answered her.

"If we land, we'll fall into the clutches of the bear. . . . And if we don't land, the current will carry us over the cataract. . . . It might be very high. . . . It could measure fifty or even a hundred feet."

"In that case, let's head for land," Nell decided. "In the meantime, grab your rifle by the barrel and whack the bear on the muzzle."

I obeyed and we glided toward the land. Suddenly, a loud cracking sound rang out, worse than the sound of revolver right in your ear. . . . I couldn't suppress a cry of terror. Nell, as silent as Bravery itself, showed me the useless handle of the broken paddle.

"Swim for it!" I cried.

"It's too late, Jerry. . . ."

The current pulled us irresistibly toward the cataract.

. . . Sitting there in the darkness and in the shadow of death, we looked at each other one last time. Even facing the unknown, I was overwhelmed by the bitterness of her passive refusal.

"Oh, Death is so cold!" shivered Nell.

. . . What a horrible memory! . . . The canoe leapt forward. It was the terrible waterfall . . . noise . . . water . . . the foam . . . the spray of the water . . . the smoke of the water . . . drizzle and vapor . . . shadows. . . .

. . . and the reawakening.

We were floating gently on very calm waves. The thunder of the cataract was now only an echo. Nell, her eyes closed, seemed to be collecting her thoughts.

My head was spinning like a child's ball. The state of stupefaction into which I was plunged was like a painful day-after hangover.

"Nell . . ." I called in a low voice.

The beautiful eyelids slowly raised themselves.

I found nothing but stupid words.

"It was a little waterfall after all. . . . If I'd only known. . . . And the bear?"

We saw it, through the yellow half-light, swimming toward the bank. The terror of this unexpected fall had taken his mind off his anger. He preferred to give up on revenge and head for the safety of the shore.

"People are idiots to say you only die once, Jerry. . . . Me, I will have gone through agony twice."

Psappha Charms the Sirens

This story draws upon Greek mythology and German folklore. The siren, which over time has merged with the folkloric figure of the mermaid (part woman, part fish), was in Greek mythology part woman and part bird. Confined to an island as punishment, the sirens lured sailors with their song to come closer to the rocky shores and risk shipwreck. In Homer's Odyssey, *Odysseus avoids this peril by stuffing up the ears of his crew and lashing himself to the mast of his ship. The sirens' danger stemmed from their charm (their singing was irresistible), and so they are an early version of the femme fatale figure. Here, Vivien explores the idea that sirens might in turn be charmed themselves, in this case by the singing of the poet Sappho, whose name she spelled Psappha according to the poet's own (Dorian) dialect.*

The Venusberg (mountain of Venus) is an otherworldly place from German medieval folk literature that blends pagan goddess worship (Venus) with Christian chivalric tradition. The story comes to be associated with the knight Tannhauser (or Tannhäuser), who starts out worshipping Venus in the mountain realm, then repents and seeks forgiveness from the Pope. When the Pope denies his petition, Tannhauser returns to Venus and her mountain home. Vivien would most likely be familiar with this tale through the work of Wagner, whose opera Tannhäuser *of 1845 foregrounded the erotic nature of the hero's time in the Venusberg. Vivien was a fan of Wagner's music and often went to Bayreuth in Germany for the annual festival of his work. Vivien may also have been aware of the extracts from the decadent artist Aubrey*

Beardsley's Under the Hill *that were published in London in the magazine* The Savoy *in 1893–94. The original manuscript, retitled* The Story of Venus and Tannhäuser, *was published for the first time in full in 1907, years after Beardsley's early death in 1898. Beardsley, too, emphasized the erotic side of the hero's adventures "under the hill." Vivien probably appreciated along with the story's erotic possibilities its accommodation of pagan gods and goddesses within the Christian realm. She liked to imagine a pre-Christian world in which homoerotic relations were accepted and there was no concept of sin.*

The incarnation of my Destiny, She who was the first to reveal me to myself, took me by the hand. She took me by the hand and led me toward the grotto where the songs of Psappha enchant the Sirens.

Just as the Goddess once hid herself in the depths of the Venusberg and reigned there despite the turning centuries and the changing universe, so these female Musicians took refuge in a Mediterranean grotto. There the blue stalactites glittered distantly like frozen stars. The sea whispered round the rocks, rocks whose green algae hair was bejeweled with anemones. A wisp of foam broke over a rock wall smoother than marble.

"Come," said the virgin incarnation of my Destiny to me. "But remember that those who enter this grotto may never return to the throng of the living.

"Like these women here, you will be forever under the spell of the Past. For you, the waves will muffle the distant bellowing of the multitude. The blue-green half-light of the evening will cause you to scorn the broad light of day. You will become estranged from the race of men. Their joys will be unknown to you; you will be indifferent to their rebukes. You will remain apart until the end of your earthly existence. You will become more dead than the radiant phantoms that surround you and who guard the uncertain survival of the Illustrious Ones. Psappha will extend to you the flower of her graces. Eranna will tell you of Agartharcis and Myro. Nossis will braid her mauve irises for you. Telesilla will sing the praises of valiant heroines for you. In her pastoral verses, Anyta will evoke for you the coolness of the fountains and the shadows of orchards. Moiro will disturb you with her enigmatic Byzantine expression. The Past, more alive and resonant than the Present, will hold you in its silvery nets. You will be held captive by dreams and by long-vanished harmonies. But you will breathe the violets of Psappha and the crocuses of Eranna of Telos. You will contemplate the white peplos worn by the virgins who bend to gather the shellfish that are as delicately mysterious as half-revealed sex organs. At times, seated on a rock, they listen to the sea-soul of the conches. Toward evening, the zither players will sing for them the songs of their native lands. Come!"

And I heard a chord that sounded like the breeze of the setting sun that sighs through pine trees at night. . . .

My strange companion took me by the hand, and I followed her into the grotto where Psappha charms the Sirens.

The Hell Club

Here Vivien adapts a work by Catherine Ann Stevens Crowe, an English author who wrote novels, plays, and short stories, including tales for children. Crowe enjoyed considerable success during her lifetime in mid-century Victorian Britain thanks in part to a successful theatrical adaptation of her novel The Adventures of Susan Hopley *(1841).* The Night Side of Nature *is a two-volume collection of supposedly true anecdotes with various supernatural themes (ghosts, premonitions, and the like) that originally appeared in 1848 but was much reprinted, translated into German and French, and widely influential. Crowe's interest in the supernatural coincided with a period of mental illness. In February 1854, for example, she was found naked and wandering the streets of Edinburgh (where she then resided), convinced that she was invisible. The story that Vivien has adapted appears toward the end of volume 1. Crowe presents the story, set in the eighteenth century, as "not a fiction, but the relation of an undoubted and well-attested fact" (356). The debauched protagonist, Mr. Archibald B. (the name Ninian appears to be Vivien's invention), has a dream in which he is afforded a vision of hell, where the innocent pleasures of earth have turned into a torture because there is no respite from them. A year and a day after the dream, as predicted, the unrepentant Archibald is discovered lying dead beside his horse. Crowe draws the moral that, while there is no harm in frivolous earthly pursuits, "if people make these things the whole business of their lives, and think of nothing else, cultivating no higher tastes, nor forming no higher aspirations, what sort of preparation are they making for another world?" (361).*

The Glasgow Hell Club,[1] we are told by the English lady author Mrs. Crowe, in a curious volume, *The Night Side of Nature*, was the talk of that fine Puritan town. The modern disciples of John Knox[2] commented severely on its orgies and shook their respectable Scottish heads in unison.

The Hell Club met every night. These evenings went on until the wee hours of the morning. And those rare passersby who were awake at first light saw, while dissembling their vague fear, the windows of the Club still lit up. The lights were softened and spectral in the vast, reproving light of dawn. Raucous songs zigzagged upward, intercut with drunken hiccups. And horrible laughter burst forth, as sinister as loveless kisses.

Every vile and abject opportunity for debauch was avidly sought out by members of the diabolical club. They were hated out of fear. They were disdained by the prudent. Everyone drew back as they insolently passed by.

The most cynical of the damned was Ninian Graham. This young Scotsman, who was neither without talents

1. In English in the original.

2. John Knox was a minister who led the Scottish Reformation and founded the Presbyterian Church of Scotland.

nor without prospects, was mired in the pleasures of vice. As soon as he came of age, he abandoned his studies for his mistresses, Barbara and Maggie, and, unable to choose between them, ruined himself impartially for both.

One November evening, Ninian set off to the mountain. His horse was valiantly following the rocky trail that skirted the abyss when a Stranger hidden behind a spectral rock came along the path and, seizing the bridle of the beast, said, "Come!" to the young Scotsman, who was frozen to the spot by uncomprehending terror.

"Where are you taking me?" stuttered Ninian finally.

"To Hell!" answered the Stranger, whose eyes were as deep as the despair of the dark.

Then the Stranger dragged Ninian down into the abyss. . . . They fell. . . . They fell for an incalculable amount of time. At last, the Stranger said, "We have arrived."

Ninian was expecting a ferocious clamor, blasphemies, and the gnashing of teeth. His sweaty brow froze. His eyelids fluttered, then closed again over his unseeing eyes.

A murmur of voices woke him from his wretched stupor. Violently, he opened his dazed eyes.

. . . He was in the house of his aunt, who had been dead five or six years. The venerable old lady was knitting, while her usual guests of days gone by, an old naval officer, a retired merchant, and his respectable spouse, all played bezique.[3] Ninian recognized them all. He shivered. They had that air of decency and smugness that, during their terrestrial existence, had been their principal feature.

"Where am I, then?" stammered the young man.

"In Hell," his old aunt answered, simply.

And, smiling, she turned her eyes back to her work.

An unspeakable horror overcame Ninian and gnawed him to the marrow. He bolted to the door, ran down the stairs, and hurled himself into the street.

The Presbyterian bells of a Scottish Sunday were pealing regularly. A well-dressed crowd of people was leaving church. Among them were fathers of families, important lady patrons of charities, retired grocers, and magistrates. Young women were passing by, their hair unbelievably neat. They held well-disciplined children by the hand.

"Where on earth am I?" Ninian asked one of the irreproachable wives.

"In Hell," she answered in a voice both modest and assured.

3. A trick-taking card game popular in the nineteenth century.

Ninian wandered for a long time in the busy streets. Night came on, ideally misty, and a vesperal peace hung over the houses. The young man saw the red glow of a cabaret shining through the shadows. There were men singing and drinking. Golden whiskey gleamed in their glasses and gin silvered their cups like moon water. Their fine drunken faces reassured and comforted Ninian.

"Where on earth am I?" he asked an old soak, who was cheerfully beginning an obscene ditty.

"In Hell, *damn you*,"[4] the merry fellow shot back with a hearty laugh.

His cordial demeanor gave our traveler new heart.

"I've always been told that Hell was a place of terrible torture," he remarked. "People are evidently wrong, or else, though I doubt it very much, I'm deceiving myself."

"They weren't wrong, nor are you mistaken," the drunkard interrupted. "We are very cheerful in Hell. That's why we suffer so terribly."

"But, from what I can see," Ninian objected, "all anyone does here is relive his earthly life."

"And there's the torture," the drunk replied. He paused to knock back a large glass of sunlit liquor, then resumed tearfully: "We were all souls without either

4. In English in the original.

love or future. We looked only for selfish material satisfaction. Thus we are condemned to relive our past lives for eternity. We retain, as we did in life, a clear gaze and a serene brow. We lead, as we did in life, the satisfied existence of fine and decent folk. And only we know what it is our hearts and minds. We were the decent people who, proud of their blameless pasts, judged the faults of the next person implacably. We were the well-bred people who, placidly surrounded by their own wealth, remained impervious to the suffering of others. We were the rapacious and voracious respectable people who are imitated deferentially by those around them. We were the ferocious and stupid well-bred people who observed decorum and upheld the laws. And that is why we are condemned to Eternal Punishment."

His drunken tears trickled down his violet-streaked cheeks.

"He gets depressed when he's had a few," thought Ninian.

The smoke was so thick that it shrouded the misty faces. The bitter alcohol fumes, the bad breath, the sweat, got into Ninian's throat and stifled him. . . . He tottered on his legs, trembling, staggering.

He found himself back on the moors, his head buried in the heather. His horse was grazing several feet away. The morning air whipped at his cheeks and temples.

. . . That dream was, according to all the evidence, a premonition from Heaven, since a year and a day after this strange vision, Ninian Graham died without having reformed, alas!

The mistakes of his earthly life make it impossible to hope that he was granted divine clemency. He was totally unable, or to be more precise, he had no idea how, to escape that Hell that had been so miraculously revealed to him.

THE FRIENDSHIP OF WOMEN

Of all the heavy-handed idiocies that Philistine essayists inflict on their readers, the most pernicious, I think, is this one: "Women are incapable of friendship. There has never been a David and Jonathan among women."

May I suggest that the affection of David for Jonathan has always seemed to me more passionate than brotherly? I need provide no further proof than the funeral oration of the young victor: *I am distressed for thee, my brother Jonathan: very pleasant hast thou been unto me: thy love to me was wonderful, passing the love of women.*[1]

I do not believe that these are the pallid tears of sorrowful friendship. Instead, I recognize the tears of blood of ardent widowhood.

How much more disinterested is the magnificent tenderness of Ruth the Moabite for Naomi![2] No carnal lan-

1. *The Bible*, 2 Samuel 1:26.

2. The story of Ruth the Moabite, the great-grandmother of David, and Naomi, her Israelite mother-in-law, is told in the Book of Ruth,

guishing creeps into the friendship between these two women. Naomi was no longer young. She says to herself: *I am too old to marry again.*

I know nothing as simple, beautiful, or touching as this passage:

> *Naomi said unto Ruth, Behold, thy sister-in-law is gone back unto her people, and unto her gods: return thou after thy sister-in-law. Ruth answered, Intreat me not to leave thee, or to return from following after thee: for whither thou goest I will go: and where thou lodgest, I will lodge: thy people shall be my people, and thy God, my God: Where thou diest, I will die, and there will I be buried: the Lord do so to me and more also, if ought but death part thee and me.*[3]

Just like the most beautiful music, these words leave you without words or breath before the Infinite.

When Naomi, with resignation, proposes to return alone to her native country where the Almighty is sending her *empty-handed*, Ruth the Moabite responds with that humble phrase, imploring her, *Intreat me not to leave thee, nor to return from following after thee*, which prepares,

---

part of the Hebrew Bible. Most Christian canons also include the book, placing it between Judges and 1 Samuel.

3. See Ruth 1:16–17.

like a murmuring prelude, the incomparable line with the fullness of an organ: *Whither thou goest, I will go. . . .*

No sob of passionate love has ever equaled the fervor of this selflessness. It is here that the poetry of friendship surpasses the poetry of love. It is spotless devotion, a pure passion. And this tenderness extends beyond the grave: *Where thou diest, I will die, and there will I be buried.*

Be honored then, Naomi, whose name means *beauty and sweetness*, for the friendship you inspired in your daughter-in-law, which the virgins of Israel celebrated thus: . . . *Thy daughter-in-law, which loveth thee, . . . she is better to thee than seven sons. . . .*

Indeed, the Book of Ruth is the apotheosis of magnanimous friendship, a friendship that is like the chaste fusion of souls, like snow melting into snow. . . . Friendship, the sobbing of zithers and the scent of violets. . . .

Oh, Naomis and Ruths of the future, believe me when I say that friendship is the best and sweetest aspect of Love.

Svanhild

One Act in Prose

This story appears to be Vivien's take on a common theme in folklore, the existence of maidens (note the recurrence of the theme of virginity) who are able to transform into swans and back again. Such a story is the basis of Pyotr Ilich Tchaikovsky's ballet Swan Lake *(1875–76, revived in 1895). Swan maiden stories occur in Germanic folklore such as the Grimms' fairy tales, but characters named Svanhild (or Swanhild or Swanhilde) also occur in other contexts. For example, in Norse mythology, Svanhild (daughter of Sigurd and Gudrun) was a queen of the Goths who was trampled to death by horses at the command of her jealous husband. The story forms part of the Saga of the Nibelungs. (This cycle was the inspiration for Wagner's Ring operas, and Vivien, as a great fan of Wagner's music, may have heard the name in this context.) Norway, the setting for this story, was also important to Vivien's personal mythology. Her father was from Yorkshire, a region of Britain invaded and colonized by Vikings in the ninth and tenth centuries (the city's name derives from Jórvik in Old Norse), and Vivien felt a personal connection to her Norse roots. There is also a Swanhilda character in the ballet* Coppélia *(music by Léo Delibes), which premiered in Paris in 1870, an adaptation of E. T. A. Hoffmann's story "The Sandman." There is no "swan" connection in the plot of the ballet (which focuses on love and marriage), but the part of the male lover was danced by a woman en travesti, a fact that may have earned Vivien's attention.*

The narrative arc recalls Vivien's story "Le cygne noir" ("The Black Swan"), published in Brumes de fjords *(Fjord Mists), in* *which the black swan is cast out by the other swans and tries to fly to the North. Although the swan dies in the process, its body is carried by the winds and tides to its destination, so that it is posthumously successful. This seems to be something of a personal myth for Vivien, who appears (intentionally?) to confuse the notion of a black swan with the metaphor of a "black sheep" (a person with a bad reputation), perhaps identifying with the one who is singled out and is rejected by the community. Vivien reshaped this bad reputation by reclaiming the role and casting the rejection as a sign of superiority that is misinterpreted by the majority, who fear or misunderstand it. An expanded version of the story was published in English as a stand-alone book in 1912 (*The One Black Swan*) under Vivien's birth name, Pauline Mary Tarn. It was subsequently translated back into French by Nicole Albert in 2018.*

SCENE 1

The scene is the bank of the North Fjord. There are mountains in the distance. Some young women in peasant costume form a group that moves about; they are treading on bluebells, thyme, and gentians. Standing still on a rock, Svanhild stares off into the distance.

THORUNN. What are you staring at so hard, Svanhild? And what do you come to wait for every day so silently?

SVANHILD. I'm waiting for the swans to return.

GUDRID. You know perfectly well that they haven't come back to this land since the day you were born. They stopped and rested for a long time on the roof of the house that sheltered you. For as long as the light lasted, they tarried on that mossy roof with the blue and golden flowers, and then at dusk they fled with a great beating of wings.

SVANHILD. They'll return.

BERGTHORA. It has been twenty years since they flew off to the North, and since that day, not one of us has seen them fly past.

SVANHILD. I know they'll return.

BERGTHORA. Why do you stay standing on the rock, motionless and contemplative for days at a time?

SVANHILD. I'm waiting for the wild swans to come back.

(Festive songs are heard. Some boats pass on the fjord, laden with women in sparkling costumes.)

PEASANT WOMEN, *singing.*

Don't go near the glacier,
For the cold burns like a flame.
Don't go near the snow,
For the snow blinds like the sun.

(Moving off.)

Don't stay on the peaks,
For the blue makes you dizzy.
Don't look down into the abyss,
For the abyss pulls you in like water.

HILDIGUNN. Listen to that distant music. The boats slip across the fjord with a gentle rocking. The peasant women sing while they row: they are happy.

SVANHILD. To me, their happiness would be the worst sort of agony, and my happiness would be the most dire torture for them.

GUDRID. Don't you love anything on this earth?

SVANHILD. I love whiteness.[1]

THORUNN. What gift do you hope for in the spring-time of your life?

SVANHILD. Whiteness.

ERMENTRUDE. If fate miraculously granted your wish, if the wild swans come back, what will you do?

SVANHILD. I'll follow them.

BERGTHORA. How far will you follow them?

SVANHILD. To the ends of the setting sun.

1. As elsewhere in Vivien's work, whiteness is a symbol of purity in general and of heterosexual chastity specifically.

HILDIGUNN. What's the goal of your dream?

SVANHILD. More whiteness.

SCENE 2

A Wanderer enters, her hands full of flowers, her head bare, her hair mingled with thyme and blades of grass.

THE WANDERER. The roads are wonderfully wide. I'm intoxicated by the dust along the way. I have slept on the heather and through my dreams I have breathed in the scent of the peaks. Red and violet berries have calmed my hunger and molten snow has slaked my thirst. I have gathered roses from the mountains. I have danced naked under the sun. Is there anything under the blue springtime sky more beautiful than the lizards on the rocks, the blue and mauve thistles, the glimpses of sparkling of fish, and the nuances of evening light?

SVANHILD. There is something more beautiful.

THE WANDERER. What on earth could be more beautiful?

SVANHILD. Clouds, snow, smoke, and foam.

THE WANDERER. Don't you want to be by my side, following the road that is as open as the horizon and as vast as the dawn?

SVANHILD. No.

THE WANDERER. Why not?

SVANHILD. I'm waiting for the wild swans to return.

(The woman goes joyfully on her way.)

SCENE 3

The sun is going down. The setting sun lights up the sky. The evening is gray and pale.

BERGTHORA. Evening is here. How mysterious the mountains are!

GUDRID. How strange the silence is!

HILDIGUNN. The whole universe seems to be waiting for something.

SVANHILD, *to herself.* Waiting . . . like me.

THORUNN. Death lies in wait for those who tarry in the mountains.

ASGERD. The paths are perilous when the fog rolls down from the peaks.

SVANHILD, *with a loud cry.* The swans! The swans! The swans!

ALL, *looking into the distance.* We can't see anything.

SVANHILD. The North wind blows through their wings. . . . They must have crossed the sea, as their plumage is silvery with foam. They're heading for the open sea. Their wings are fully open and flapping like sails. . . . Can you hear the generous beating of their wings?

ALL. All we can see are the white clouds floating over the fjord.

SVANHILD. They are more beautiful than clouds. They are heading for the northern lights. They are more beautiful than the snow. Their flight is so powerful and resonant! Can you hear them flying by?

ALL. All we can hear is the evening breeze over the fjord.

SVANHILD. I'm going to follow them! I'm going to follow them to the ends of the setting sun!

ASGERD. Svanhild! The paths are perilous when the fog rolls down from the peaks.

THORUNN. Death lies in wait for those who tarry in the mountains.

GUDRID. Beware of the mists that hide the abyss.

SVANHILD. Oh, whiteness!

(She flees into the thick of the fog.)

ASGERD. She'll get lost in the twilight.

GUDRID. She'll perish in the night. Svanhild!

ALL, *calling*. Svanhild!

ECHO. Svanhild!

(A loud cry taken up by an echo is heard.)

GUDRID, *anxiously*. The abyss. . . .

White as Foam

In Greek mythology, Andromeda is an Ethiopian princess who pays the price for her mother's pride. As punishment for her mother's boasts about her daughter's beauty, Andromeda is chained to a rock to be sacrificed to the appetites (gastronomic, but also, it is often implied, sexual) of a sea monster. Andromeda is saved at the eleventh hour by Perseus, slayer of the Gorgon Medusa, on his winged horse Pegasus. The subject of a maiden saved from a monster or dragon by a hero on horseback became a popular theme from the Middle Ages on, and the depiction of a vulnerable, naked or scantily clad virgin squirming in chains was also irresistible to many painters throughout the ages. Vivien's insistence on Andromeda's whiteness here merits comment. Since Andromeda was Ethiopian, a darker skin color is more likely, but we should perhaps interpret Vivien's insistence on whiteness not as a racial trait, but as a reference to moral and sexual purity (and thus related to virginity).

White as foam on the gray of the rocks, Andromeda gazed at the sea. In her face burned the desire for Space.

Under the weight of her golden chains, her delicate limbs soaked up the sunlight. The wind of the open sea blew through her free-flowing hair. The sounds of the sea's laughter reached her ears, and the dazzle of the shimmering waves penetrated her soul.

She was waiting for Death; she waited, white as foam on the gray of the rocks.

She felt herself already lost in the infinite, one with the horizon and with the gold-flecked waves, with the distant mists, with the air itself and with the resounding clarity of the whole. Not in the least did she fear chaste-eyed, solemn-handed Death; what she feared was Love, ravager of spirit and of flesh.

White as foam on the gray of the rocks, she dreamed that the merciful Gods, by delivering her virginal self to virginal Death, would spare her the rancors and defilements of implacable Eros.

Suddenly, her dilated eyes focused on the Sea Monster who was coming from the depths toward his motionless prey, his royal victim.

His aqueous scales were dripping with blue and green water and glistened with shimmers and rays of light. He was magnificent and formidable. And his huge eyes contained the depths of the Ocean that rocked him with its rhythms and its dreams.

A sob of terror and love burst from Andromeda's lips. Her eyelids fluttered before they closed in the face of the voluptuousness of his look. Her lips savored the bitter taste of Death.

. . . But the hour of deliverance had sounded and the Hero appeared, armed by the Parthenian[1] and looking like summer lightning. The battle took place in the waves and Perseus's sword was victorious. The Monster sank slowly into the shadows of the water.

As the victor went to break the golden chains of the Captive, he was stopped by the silent reproach of her tears.

Andromeda's voice slowly sobbed, "Why couldn't you let me perish in a grand gesture of Sacrifice? The beauty of my incomparable Destiny was intoxicating, and now you have torn me away from Lethe's kiss. O Perseus, you should know that my only sob of desire was for the Sea Monster, and that Death seemed to me less oppressive than your imminent embrace."

1. Perseus was under the protection of the goddess Athena, whose temple was the Parthenon (the temple of virgins) in Athens.

Bona Dea

It is the dying of the day. It is that evening in the spring dedicated to the Great Goddess.[1] Cover up the picture of my father with an opaque veil so that the gaze of the Immortal Virgin will not be offended by the sight of a man.

Tonight my father's house will be the temple where the sacred rites will be carried out. . . .

How beautiful she is, this statue of the Daughter of Faunus![2] Bona Dea, deign to look down smilingly on our choirs and on our offerings.

I braided the crown of violets for your brow myself. . . . Your marble brow is so vast and solemn, o Goddess!

Here is the golden vessel into which I have poured the wine from Lesbos. The wine is as luminous as Peitho's

1. The "Great Goddess" refers to the Bona Dea (literally, the "good goddess"), an ancient Roman goddess.

2. Faunus was the ancient Roman god of nature, the forests, and the wild. He came to be identified with the Greek god Pan. Like Pan, Faunus was depicted as part animal, having horns and the legs of a goat.

hair.[3] It is purple like the mantle of Apollo. It will gladden the dancing soul of the intertwined women.

. . . Thrice-precious Amata, close your beautiful eyelids that are like dark flowers. Abandon your childlike hands to my ardent ones.

I love you. I, Caia Venantia Paullina, daughter of Caius Venantius Paullinus, I love you, my little Gallic slave. You were but a wretched and graceless child, and the merchants disdained you. But I cherished you immediately and fervently for your lassitude and fragility. I opened my arms to you, as much to console as to embrace you. . . .

For I am the one who rules and protects. I love you with a sweet and imperious love. I love you like a lover and like a sister. You will obey me, my sweet care, but you can do with me what you will. I'll be both your master and your thing. I love you with the fury of male desire and the languor of feminine tenderness.

. . . Once I used to open my arms to you as much to console as to embrace you. Your trembling nudity, which I didn't yet covet, charmed me with its candor. I loved you for being frail and trembling. My strength was attracted to your weakness. For I am the one who rules and protects.

3. Peitho was the goddess of persuasion and seduction in Greek mythology.

And now you are beautiful, Amata. Your breasts, like polished stones, are firm and cool to the touch. Your green eyes reflect the emerald green foliage of oak trees. Your body has the white transparency of pearls of mistletoe.[4] Your flowing hair has the splendor of forests in October.

And because you are beautiful, Amata, because you are the most gracious of adolescents, I am going to reveal to you the power and sweetness of female love.

If you will grant me your consenting body, I'll teach you the multifaceted art of Pleasure. I'll teach you the clever slowness of hands that prolong the feel of their lingering strokes. I'll teach you the tenacity of lips that cling delicately. You'll experience the all-powerful lightness of touch.

When you were still only a wretched and graceless child, I taught you the Odes of Sappho of Lesbos, whose beautiful name is Psappha in Dorian. You should know, my beautiful slave, that because I am her priestess, Psappha, who lies among the lotuses of Lethe, smiles when I say her name and protects my love affairs. She'll help me to overcome and hold onto your hesitating heart, Amata.

---

4. The mistletoe plant, whose white berries are referred to here, was thought to have a special role in certain pre-Christian European cults, such as those of the druids.

I love you the way Psappha used to love Atthis, who was elusive and unsure.

. . . And because you are the most graceful of adolescents, Amata, I'll show you the power and sweetness of women's love.

You're free, o my beautiful slave! Here's the linen dress I wove for you. . . . It's white, Amata, it's almost as attractive to touch as your very body. You're free. You can cross the threshold of this house that sheltered your childhood. You can return to your own country, and I won't say a word of blame or utter a single reproach; I won't darken your joy with the slightest complaint.

For love between women is nothing like the love of men. I love you for you, and not for me. All I want from you is the smile of your lips and the light of your eyes.

Why am I beautiful in your eyes? For you are the beautiful one, not me. My hair doesn't have the evening gold that yours does. My eyes don't have the faraway brightness that yours do. My lips don't have the chiseled definition yours do. Truly, you are the beautiful one, not me.

I never saw a young girl as desirable as you, o my voluptuous one, o my langorous one! . . . Next to you, I'm not beautiful at all. If some other desirable virgin pleases you more, take her. All I want is the smile on your lips.

I love you.

My pearls will look more lustrous around your neck. My beryls will be clearer on your arm. Take my necklaces. Take my rings too. That way, you'll be dressed for the feast of Bona Dea.

She is simple and sweet and merciful toward women. She hates men, because man is ferocious and brutal. Man loves only his pride and bestiality. He is neither just nor loyal. He is sincere only in his vanity. But the Goddess is all truth and justice. She is as full of pity as water that refreshes lips and sun that warms limbs. She is the clement Soul of the universe.

She it is who caused the first flowers to grow. Flowers are a work of love by the Great Goddess, the mark of her favor toward mortal women.

She loves only women's faces. No man must sully with his presence the venerable temple where she gives her oracles. And the female priestesses are the only ones who have heard the divine sound of her voice.

She is the Daughter of Faunus. She is the chaste and prophetic Fauna. Her mysterious name must never be uttered by the profane lips of a man, but I'll tell you secretly what it is: it's Oma. You must never divulge this secret name.

It is the dying of the day. It is that evening in the spring dedicated to the Great Goddess. With their own hands, the Vestals have tied garlands on the walls now scented by the foliage.

Doesn't it look like a still forest? . . . The last glimmers of light linger on her pale hair. . . . You look like a Hamadryad framed by shade and greenery. . . .

With their own hands, the Vestals have tied garlands on the walls now scented by the foliage. They have chosen simple flowers and the herbs that are most dear to Fauna: balm, thyme, chervil, fennel, and parsley. And here are hyacinths. . . . Here, roses. . . .

The Great Goddess is gladdened by the joy of the universe. Compassionate nymphs serve and honor her, nymphs who, in the feverish heat of summer, bring a water sweeter than honey cupped in their hands. . . .

The Goddess has colored the apples scarlet. She has made the virginal crocuses of the garden white. She has turned the nocturnal blue of violets to purple.

Fauna smiles at the love of intertwined women. That's why, when night comes, women will put their lips together in front of her beautiful statue, expertly molded by Theano the Greek. The hair is a mass of gold, the limbs are ivory, and the eyes are emerald. . . . But your hair is even more luminous, your limbs more polished, your eyes a deeper green. . . .

My fervent hands have bound her divine forehead with vine leaves. . . . A serpent is coiled around her delicate feet. . . . For she is Eternal Sweetness and also Eternal Wisdom.

The wives who will come this evening have purified themselves by refusing the embrace of their husbands. But they are less dear to the Goddess than the sacred virgins.

Here is the night, azure like the veil that protects the Divine Image, and that must be raised only by the hands of Priestesses. For the Goddess reveals herself only on the spring evening when intertwined women piously unite.

Come, Amata, my beautiful slave. If you love me even a little, you'll allow me the kiss that my lips anxiously await from your lips. You'll bend to my willful embrace. You'll abandon yourself to my imploring caress. . . .

But I won't bother you with my desire or my tenderness, Beloved. . . . All I want is the smile of your lips.

Works Cited in Headnotes and Footnotes

Adler, Laure. *La vie quotidienne dans les maisons closes: 1830–1930.* Hachette, 1990.

Albert, Nicole G., and Brigitte Rollet, editors. *Renée Vivien: Une femme de lettres entre deux siècles, 1877–1909.* Champion, 2012.

The Bible. Authorized King James Version. Oxford UP, 2008.

Crowe, Catherine. *The Night Side of Nature; or, Ghosts and Ghost Seers.* Vol. 1, T. C. Newby, 1849.

Datta, Venita. *Heroes and Legends of Fin-de-Siècle France: Gender, Politics, and National Identity.* Cambridge UP, 2011.

Doniger, Wendy. *The Bedtrick: Tales of Sex and Masquerade.* U of Chicago P, 2000.

———. *The Woman Who Pretended to Be Who She Was: Myths of Self-Imitation.* Oxford UP, 2006.

Dumas, Alexandre. *Le meneur de loups.* 1857.

Garfield, Simon. *Mauve: How One Man Invented a Color that Changed the World.* W. W. Norton, 2001.

Goujon, Jean-Paul. "Renée Vivien et les éditions Lemerre (d'après des lettres inédites)." *Renée Vivien à rebours: Études pour un centenaire,* edited by Nicole Albert, Orizons, 2009, pp. 43–54.

Hawthorne, Melanie. "Des antécédents américains de Renée Vivien." *Histoires Littéraires,* no. 66, 2016, pp. 69–74.

———. "Two Nice Girls." *Dix-Neuf,* vol. 21, no. 1, 2017, pp. 69–92, https://doi.org/10.1080/14787318.2017.1285132.

Pougy, Liane de. *Idylle saphique.* La Plume, 1901.

Rosello, Mireille. *Infiltrating Culture: Power and Identity in Contemporary Women's Writing.* Manchester UP, 1996.

Sante, Luc. *The Other Paris: The People's City, Nineteenth and Twentieth Centuries.* Farrar, Straus and Giroux, 2015.

Smith, Jay M. *Monsters of the Gévaudan: The Making of a Beast.* Harvard UP, 2011.

Stoker, Bram. *Dracula*. 1897.

Vivien, Renée. "The Black Swan." *Lilith's Legacy: Prose Poems and Short Stories*, by Vivien, translated by Brian Stableford, Snuggly Books, 2018, pp. 7–8.

———. "Le cygne noir." *Brumes de fjords*, by Vivien, Alphonse Lemerre, 1902, pp. 13–15.

———. *Le cygne noir / The One Black Swan*. Edited and translated by Nicole Albert, Éditions ÉrosOnyx, 2018.

———. *Les kitharèdes*. Éditions ÉrosOnyx, 2008.

——— [*published as* Pauline Mary Tarn]. *The One Black Swan*. Constable, 1912.

Notes on Contributors

Melanie Hawthorne is professor of French at Texas A&M University. She has previously worked on the decadent French author Rachilde (whose *Monsieur Vénus* is included in the MLA Texts and Translations series). Hawthorne has published articles on Renée Vivien and is currently at work on a biography.

Karla Jay is distinguished professor emerita at Pace University in New York City. She has written, edited, and translated ten books, the most recent of which is *Tales of the Lavender Menace: A Memoir of Liberation*. She is also the author of *The Amazon and the Page: Natalie Clifford Barney and Renée Vivien* and the recipient of many awards, including the Bill Whitehead Award for Lifetime Achievement in Writing.

Yvonne M. Klein is retired from Dawson College, Montreal, where she was a professor of English. She has translated a number of books in French by Canadian authors, both fiction and nonfiction, including several novels by Jovette Marchessault. One of these, *Lesbian Triptych*, won the Canada Council's prize for best translation.